The Secret Garden

祕密花園

Original Author   Frances Hodgson Burnett
Adaptor   David Desmond O'Flaherty
Illustrator   Petra Hanzak

WORDS
600

MP3

Let's Enjoy Masterpieces!

All the beautiful fairy tales and masterpieces that you have encountered during your childhood remain as warm memories in your adulthood. This time, let's indulge in the world of masterpieces through English. You can enjoy the depth and beauty of original works, which you can't enjoy through Chinese translations.

The stories are easy for you to understand because of your familiarity with them. When you enjoy reading, your ability to understand English will also rapidly improve.

This series of *Let's Enjoy Masterpieces* is a special reading comprehension booster program, devised to improve reading comprehension for beginners whose command of English is not satisfactory, or who are elementary, middle, and high school students. With this program, you can enjoy reading masterpieces in English with fun and efficiency.

This carefully planned program is composed of 5 levels, from the beginner level of 350 words to the intermediate and advanced levels of 1,000 words. With this program's level-by-level system, you are able to read famous texts in English and to savor the true pleasure of the world's language.

The program is well conceived, composed of reader-friendly explanations of English expressions and grammar, quizzes to help the student learn vocabulary and understand the meaning of the texts, and fabulous illustrations that adorn every page. In addition, with our "Guide to Listening," not only is reading comprehension enhanced but also listening comprehension skills are highlighted.

In the audio recording of the book, texts are vividly read by professional American voice actors. The texts are rewritten, according to the levels of the readers by an expert editorial staff of native speakers, on the basis of standard American English with the ministry of education recommended vocabulary. Therefore, it will be of great help even for all the students that want to learn English.

Please indulge yourself in the fun of reading and listening to English through *Let's Enjoy Masterpieces*.

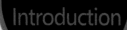

法蘭西絲・霍森・伯內特

Frances Hodgson Burnett
(1849–1924)

Frances Hodgson Burnett was an American writer. She was born in Manchester, England. After her father's death when she was three years old, the family moved to America. To earn money for her family by writing, Burnett sent in a story. Then, as the story was adopted, she began her writing career in earnest.

In 1886, she published *The Little Lord Fauntleroy*, modeled after her second son. Following the great success of *The Little Lord Fauntleroy*, Burnett wrote *Sara Crew* (later rewritten to become: *A Little Princess*) and *Secret Garden*, which she is best known for today.

Drawing upon her own experiences, where she never gave up her dreams and hopes, and despite many obstacles, Burnett created characters who endure hardships and tribulations with optimism and courage.

Burnett is credited for making a turning point in American children's literature, when most stories written for children were designed to convey moral advice. Still widely loved as beautiful and lovely stories, Burnett's works have reached the status of all-time classics of children's literature.

Published in 1911, *The Secret Garden* is one of the excellent books written by Burnett. *The Secret Garden* tells the story of the process of the regeneration of two hurt and abandoned children finding the path to spiritual health, as they tend flowers in a walled garden that has been neglected and left in ruins.

Distraught over the loss of his wife, Mr. Craven, living in a manor in England, locks up the garden that his wife adored, and nobody is allowed to enter it. Then one day, the long-abandoned garden is discovered by Mary, a little orphaned girl who didn't cry after losing her parents, Colin, an invalid, bed-ridden, wheelchair-bound boy, and Dickon, a robust country boy nourished by the natural surroundings of the countryside.

The three children work hard to nurse the deserted garden back to life, and finally the garden is transformed into a paradise, blossoming full of life with plants and animals. The sickly Colin recovers his health and begins to walk. Mr. Craven, who had been mired in grief after his wife's death, becomes overjoyed to find that his son has become healthy.

HOW TO USE THIS BOOK

本書使用說明

1 Original English texts

It is easy to understand the meaning of the text, because the text is rewritten according to the levels of the readers.

2 Explanation of the vocabulary

The words and expressions that include vocabulary above the elementary level are clearly defined.

3 Response notes

Spaces are included in the book so you can take notes about what you don't understand or what you want to remember.

4 One point lesson

In-depth analyses of major grammar points and expressions help you to understand sentences with difficult grammar.

🎧 *Audio Recording*

In the audio recording, native speakers narrate the texts in standard American English. By combining the written words and the audio recording, you can listen to English with great ease.

Audio books have been popular in Britain and America for many decades. They allow the listener to experience the proper word pronunciation and sentence intonation that add important meaning and drama to spoken English. Students will benefit from listening to the recording twenty or more times.

After you are familiar with the text and recording, listen once more with your eyes closed to check your listening comprehension. Finally, after you can listen with your eyes closed and understand every word and every sentence, you are then ready to mimic the native speaker.

Then you should make a recording by reading the text yourself. Then play both recordings to compare your oral skills with those of a native speaker.

HOW TO IMPROVE
READING ABILITY

如何增進英文閱讀能力

① *Catch key words*

Read the key words in the sentences and practice catching the gist of the meaning of the sentence. You might question how working with a few important words could enhance your reading ability. However, it's quite effective.   If you continue to use this method, you will find out that the key words and your knowledge of people and situations enables you to understand the sentence.

② *Divide long sentences*

Read in chunks of meaning, dividing sentences into meaningful chunks of information. In the book, chunks are arranged in sentences according to meaning. If you consider the sentences backwards or grammatically, your reading speed will be slow and you will find it difficult to listen to English.

You are ready to move to a more sophisticated level of comprehension when you find that narrowly focusing on chunks is irritating. Instead of considering the chunks, you will make it a habit to read the sentence from the beginning to the end to figure out the meaning of the whole.

③ *Make inferences and assumptions*

Making inferences and assumptions are part of your ability. If you don't know, try to guess the meaning of the words. Although you don't know all the words in context, don't go straight to the dictionary. Developing an ability to make inferences in the context is important.

The first way to figure out the meaning of a word is from its context. If you cannot make head or tail out of the meaning of a word, look at what comes before or after it. Ask yourself what can happen in such a situation. Make your best guess as to the word's meaning. Then check the explanations of the word in the book or look up the word in a dictionary.

④ *Read a lot and reread the same book many times*

There is no shortcut to mastering English. Only if you do a lot of reading will you make your way to the summit. Read fun and easy books with an average of less than one new word per page. Try to immerse yourself in English as often as you can.

Spend time "swimming" in English. Language learning research has shown that immersing yourself in English will help you improve your English, even though you may not be aware of what you're learning.

CONTENTS

Before You Read

Mary

My name is Mary Lennox. I grew up in India. My parents are dead, so I live with my uncle in a huge castle. Most days you can find me working hard in my secret garden. This is a very special place, where I can meet friends, play with the animals, and enjoy nature.

Dickon

Hi, I'm Dickon. I love animals. They are my friends. I spend most of my time in the gardens at Misselthwaite Manor. Gardening is my favorite pastime. I think everyone should be outside working in gardens.

Colin

I'm Colin Craven, Archibald Craven's son. I'm very sick, so I spend most of my time alone, in bed. I read a lot but I wish I had friends to talk to and to play with outside.
I forget what having fun is like.

Archibald Craven

My name is Archibald Craven. Sadly, my wife died ten years ago in our garden. I travel all over the world, so I don't have time to see my son. I don't mean to be a bad father—it's just that seeing my son reminds me how much I miss my wife.

Chapter One

Mary Lennox

Mary Lennox had a thin little face and a thin little body, thin light[1] hair and a very sour[2] expression[3]. She never smiled—not once during the long trip to England.

She had come from India where a terrible disease[4] had killed thousands of people. Among the dead were Mary's mother and father. She didn't miss[5] them very much since[6] she hardly[7] knew them. Her parents were always away somewhere for important business. Mary Lennox hardly even knew what their faces looked like.

1. **light** [laɪt] (a.) 淺色的
2. **sour** [saʊr] (a.) 脾氣壞的
3. **expression** [ɪkˋspreʃən] (n.) 臉色；表情
4. **disease** [dɪˋziːz] (n.) 疾病
5. **miss** [mɪs] (v.) 想念
6. **since** [sɪns] (conj.) 因為；由於
7. **hardly** [ˋhɑːrdli] (adv.) 幾乎不

Among **the dead** were Mary's mother and father.
在喪生的人當中有瑪麗的父母親。

Mary's mother and father were among **the dead**.
瑪麗的父母親在喪生名單中。

---

the + (adj.)：有一些形容詞常與定冠詞 the 連用，構成複數名詞。

e.g. the rich 富有的人　the poor 貧窮的人

Instead of parents, Mary had servants[1] that took care of[2] her. She only needed to ask people for whatever she needed. Unfortunately, Mary grew up believing that everybody was her servant.

Now that[3] Mary's parents were dead, the girl had only one relative[4]. His name was Mr. Archibald Craven. Mary didn't know anything about the man. But she would live in his house until she was eighteen years old.

When Mary finally arrived in England, Mrs. Medlock, Archibald Craven's housekeeper[5], met her at the port[6].

"Are you my servant?" Mary asked.

"Hmmm!" grunted[7] Mrs. Medlock. "You'd better mind[8] your manners[9]! I work for your uncle. Not for you! I'm supposed to[10] bring you to Yorkshire[11]. That's where your new home will be. Follow[12] me. We have to catch the two o'clock train. Hurry up!"

On the train, Mary mostly just stared out the window and watched the English landscape [13] roll by [14]. How different it seemed from India!

1. **servant** [ˋsɜːrvənt] (n.) 僕人
2. **take care of** 照顧；處理
3. **now that** 既然
4. **relative** [ˋrelətɪv] (n.) 親戚
5. **housekeeper** [ˋhaʊsˌkiːpər] (n.) 管家
6. **port** [pɔːrt] (n.) 港口
7. **grunt** [grʌnt] (v.) 咕噥著說
8. **mind** [maɪnd] (v.) 注意；留意
9. **manners** [ˋmænərz] (n.) 態度；舉止
10. **be supposed to** 應該……
11. **Yorkshire** 約克郡（英格蘭東北的一郡）
12. **follow** [ˋfɑːloʊ] (v.) 跟隨
13. **landscape** [ˋlændskeɪp] (n.) 景色
14. **roll by** 消逝

"Wake up, dear[1]. We've arrived. It's time to go to Misselthwaite Manor," said Mrs. Medlock.

"What's 'Misselthwaite Manor?'"

"That's the name of your new home. It's a huge[2] castle[3] that has belonged to[4] the Craven family for hundreds of years. It has a very big lake beside it and many gardens. There are a hundred rooms in the house. Most of them are locked[5], though."

1. **dear** [dɪr] (a.) 親愛的
2. **huge** [hju:dʒ] (a.) 巨大的
3. **castle** [ˋkæsəl] (n.) 城堡
4. **belong to** 屬於⋯⋯
5. **lock** [lɑ:k] (v.) 鎖上
6. **crooked** [ˋkrukɪd] (a.) 彎腰曲背的
7. **set** [set] (v.) 使處於
8. **nowadays** [ˋnauədeɪz] (adv.) 現今；當下
9. **once in a while** 有時
10. **either** [ˋi:ðər] (adv.) (用於否定句) 也

"Why are they locked?" Mary asked.

"Mr. Craven likes it that way."

"Why?"

"Well, it's a long story. Mr. Craven is a crooked[6] man. That set[7] him wrong. He was a sour young man until he was married. His wife was very beautiful, and he loved her very much.

When she died he became even stranger. He locked himself in his room for months. Nowadays[8], he comes out once in a while[9]. But he hardly ever meets people. I'm sure he won't meet you, either[10]."

One Point Lesson

• It's a huge castle that **has belonged** to the Craven family **for** hundreds of years.
  這個大城堡是屬於克萊文家的，已經有數百年之久。

have+ 過去分詞：現在簡單完成式是用以銜接過去和現在的時態，強調在某方面與現在有關的過去動作或事件。表示「時間持續多久」要用 for 來連接。

e.g I **have lived** here in London **for** ten years.
   我住在倫敦這裡已經有十年了。

🎧 4

When they arrived at Misselthwaite Manor, Mary couldn't believe her eyes. The castle was bigger than anything she'd ever seen or imagined. The gardens surrounding[1] the castle were beautiful, even though[2] the flowers weren't blooming[3] yet.

"Come on, Mary. I'll show you to your room," said Mrs. Medlock. Mary was led[4] up three staircases[5] and down a long corridor[6] to her room. Inside, a fire was burning in the fireplace[7] and a table was set with a delicious[8] supper[9].

"This is your room, Mary. You must stay in here while you're in the house. Outside, you can go wandering[10] as much as you like."

"Yes, ma'am[11]," Mary said. As the girl sat down to supper, she felt more lonely[12] than she had ever felt before.

1. **surround** [səˋraʊnd] (v.) 圍繞;圈住
2. **even though** 即使;雖然
3. **bloom** [blum] (v.) 開花
4. **lead** [liːd] (v.) 引導;領路
5. **staircase** [ˋsterkeɪs] (n.) 樓梯
6. **corridor** [ˋkɔːrɪdər] (n.) 走廊
7. **fireplace** [ˋfaɪrpleɪs] (n.) 壁爐
8. **delicious** [dɪˋlɪʃəs] (a.) 美味的
9. **supper** [ˋsʌpər] (n.) 晚餐
10. **wander** [ˋwɑːndər] (v.) 漫遊
11. **ma'am** [mæm] (n.) 夫人;女士
12. **lonely** [ˋloʊnli] (a.) 孤獨的

Outside, you can go wandering **as much as you like.**
在外面，你喜歡閒晃多久都可以。

---

as much as + 主詞 + 動詞：……那麼多（much 修飾的詞為不可數名詞）。**as many as** 修飾的詞為可數名詞。

You can get **as many books** as you want.
你想要拿幾本書都可以。

🎧 5

The next morning, Mary was woken up[1] by a maid[2] named[3] Martha.

"It's time to get up now," said Martha, with a big smile. "Come on, get dressed[4]."

"I don't know how to[5] dress myself[6]."

"Then, it's time you should learn."

1. **wake up** 喚醒
   (wake-woke-woken)
2. **maid** [meɪd] (n.) 女僕
3. **name** [neɪm] (v.) 被稱為
4. **get dressed** 穿衣
5. **how to**
   如何……（後接原型動詞）
6. **dress oneself** 自己穿衣
7. **eat up** 吃完
8. **by oneself** 單獨地
9. **from now on** 從現在開始

Mary was shocked a little, but dressed herself for the first time in her life.

Martha brought her a big breakfast.

"You eat up[7], now. Then, go outside and play."

"Won't you come and play with me?" Mary asked.

"No. You'll have to play by yourself[8] from now on[9]. If you're lucky[10], maybe you'll run into[11] my little brother, Dickon."

"Dickon?"

"Yes. Dickon's a little boy who makes friends with[12] animals."

"Where can I find Dickon?" Mary asked.

"Oh, he's usually around somewhere. You'll probably find him in the gardens."

10. **lucky** [ˋlʌki] (a.) 幸運的
11. **run into** 跑進 (run-ran-run)
12. **make friends with**
    和……交朋友

23

"What gardens?"

Martha laughed. "You're full of[1] questions, aren't you? I mean[2] the gardens surrounding the manor. There are quite[3] a few of them. But there's one you can't go into. It's locked up."

"Why is it locked?"

"Well, that's where Mrs. Craven died ten years ago. She climbed up[4] into a tree one day and then fell out of it. After that, Mr. Craven locked the gate to the garden and buried[5] the key."

Mary liked the idea of a secret garden. It sounded[6] strange and exciting to her.

"You go and play now," said Martha.

As Mary walked outside, she could see tall trees all around. There also were flower beds[7] and evergreens[8] clipped[9] into strange shapes.

There were no leaves on trees, however, and the flowers were not blooming yet.

1. **be full of** 充滿……
2. **mean** [miːn] 意指;意謂 (mean-meant-meant)
3. **quite** [kwaɪt] (adv.) 相當
4. **climb up** 爬上
5. **bury** [`beri] (v.) 埋葬
6. **sound** [saʊnd] (v.) 聽起來
7. **flower bed** 花圃
8. **evergreen** [`ɛvərgriːn] (n.) 常綠樹
9. **clip** [klɪp] (v.) 修剪
10. **however** [haʊ`ɛvər] (conj.) 然而;不過

♦ There were no leaves on trees, **however**, and the flowers were not blooming yet.

然而，樹上沒有樹葉，花兒也還沒開。

---

however：然而；不過（however 當句子副詞時，可放在句首、主詞和動詞之間，或句尾。

e.g. However, this is my job. 然而，這是我的工作。

Later, **however**, he told the truth.

不過，之後他告訴了我事實。

Walking down one path[1], Mary noticed[2] one wall that was covered in ivy[3], but seemed to have no door in it. She could see tall trees behind the wall.

"There must be a gate along here somewhere," Mary said.

At that moment, Mary heard a robin[4] singing in one of the trees above her. As she looked up, she noticed it jumping between branches[5]. It seemed as if[6] it was trying to get her attention[7]. It's cheerful[8] whistle[9] brought a small smile to her sad face.

As Mary returned to Misselthwaite Manor, she began to think a lot about the secret garden. She felt that the garden must be beyond[10] the wall that she had walked along.

1. **path** [pæθ] (n.) 小路
2. **notice** [`noutɪs] (v.) 注意；注意到
3. **ivy** [`aɪvi] (n.) 常春藤
4. **robin** [`rɑːbɪn] (n.) 知更鳥
5. **branch** [bræntʃ] (n.) 樹枝
6. **seem as if** 似乎好像
7. **attention** [ə`tenʃən] (n.) 注意力
8. **cheerful** [`tʃɪrfəl] (a.) 愉快的；興高采烈的
9. **whistle** [`wɪsəl] (n.) 鳥鳴聲
10. **beyond** [bɪ`jɑːnd] (prep.) 更遠於

That night, as[1] Mary sat in bed thinking about the secret garden, she heard a strange sound. At first[2], she thought it was the wind howling[3]. But then she noticed that the sound was coming from[4] inside the castle. It sounded like a boy crying.

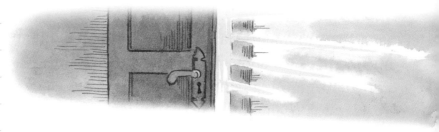

Mary walked out of[5] her room and knocked[6] on Martha's door.

"Martha! Martha!" she called. "I think I hear a boy crying."

Martha opened the door and said, "Nonsense[7]. It's just the wind."

"But the sound is coming from inside the house."

"No, it's not. Now you go to bed right now[8]."

1. **as** [əz] (conj.) 當⋯⋯時
2. **at first** 首先
3. **howl** [haʊl] (v.) 怒吼；狂叫
4. **come from** 來自⋯⋯
5. **out of** 自⋯⋯離開

That night, Mary had two dreams. One dream was a happy one. It was about a secret garden with roses and wild flowers[9] blooming.

The other dream wasn't so happy. It was about a boy crying in a room with no mother or father to take care of him.

6. **knock** [nɑːk] (v.) 敲擊
7. **nonsense** [ˋnɑːnsens] (n.) 胡說
8. **right now** 即刻；現在
9. **wild flower** 野花

A True or False.

1 Mary had come from India.   T F

2 In India, Mary often dressed herself.   T F

3 When Mary arrived in England, she thought   T F
that everyone was her servant.

4 Archibald Craven was Mary's father.   T F

5 Mary never felt lonely at Misselthwaite Manor.   T F

6 Mary didn't care very much about the   T F
secret garden.

B Match.

1 Beside the house   •   • A were not blooming yet.

2 Mary dreamed about   •   • B there was a big lake.

3 There are a   •   • C a boy crying. hundred rooms

4 The flowers   •   • D in Misselthwaite Manor.

5 Ten years ago   •   • E Mr. Craven's beautiful wife died.

C Choose the correct answer.

1 Why did Mr. Craven lock himself into his room?

(a) Because his wife died and he was shy.

(b) Because his wife died and he was sad.

(c) Because his wife died and he was poor.

2 What would happen when the weather got warmer?

(a) Mary would find a secret garden.

(b) The trees in the orchard would have fruit on them.

(c) Flowers would start to bloom.

D Rearrange the sentences in chronological order.

1 Mary was sent to England to live with her uncle.

2 Everyone in the house, except for Mary, died of a terrible disease.

3 Mary's uncle didn't want to see her.

4 Mary lived in India with her mother and father.

5 Mary traveled by train to Yorkshire.

_____ ⇨ _____ ⇨ _____ ⇨ _____ ⇨ _____

English Children in India

When Mary Lennox arrived at Misselthwaite Manor, she was a very rude child. Her bad behavior is a reflection of the way she was raised in India. In 1911, the time that Frances Hodgson Burnett wrote *The Secret Garden*, Britain controlled all of India. Hundreds of British people, like Mary's parents, went to India to help govern the country.

Most of them lived like kings with many Indian servants who did everything for them. The British children of these families must have felt like little princes and princesses.

They were looked after by Indian servants who had to do anything that the children asked. These servants even put on the children's clothes for them! It was not surprising that some of these children became spoiled and lazy.

However, these children may also have felt neglected by their parents. Usually the parents were too busy with their jobs or social lives to spend time with their own children.

New Delhi

India

Chapter Two

🎧 ⁹ Way to the Secret Garden

Everyday, Mary always did the same things. After breakfast, Mary would¹ walk in the gardens. Often, she would hear the sound of the boy crying at night. But she was always told that it was just the wind.

One day, as Mary was walking in the gardens, she smelled something wet and muddy². It smelled like something living.

"Springtime³ is coming," she said aloud⁴.

Suddenly, Mary heard a bird call over her shoulder. It was the robin that Mary had seen on her first day at the manor.

1. **would** [wʊd] (aux.) 總是;總會
2. **muddy** [ˋmʌdi] (a.) 多爛泥的;泥濘的
3. **springtime** (n.) 春天
4. **aloud** [əˋlaʊd] (adv.) 大聲地
5. **toward** [tuˋwɔːrdz] (prep.) 向;朝
6. **expect** [ɪkˋspekt] (v.) 期待;盼望
7. **rusty** [ˋrʌsti] (a.) 生鏽的
8. **ring** [rɪŋ] (n.) 環;圈

Mary walked toward[5] the bird. It didn't fly away, as Mary expected[6] it to.

The bird was standing on a rusty[7] ring[8] on a small mound[9] of earth. It looked like maybe a dog had been digging[10] there. Mary pulled the ring out of the hole[11].

"What's this?" she cried. A key was attached[12] to the ring.

9. **mound** [maʊnd] (n.) 土石堆
10. **dig** [dɪg] (v.) 挖掘
    (dig-dug-dug)

11. **hole** [hoʊl] (n.) 洞
13. **attach** [əˋtætʃ] (v.)
    使依附；使附著

One Point Lesson

But she **was** always **told** that it was just the wind.
但別人總是告訴她說那只是風。

be told：被告知（這裡為被動式，told 是 tell 的過去分詞。）

e.g. They **were told** to use a pencil instead of a pen.
他們被告知要用鉛筆來代替鋼筆。

Mary felt very excited[1] all of a sudden[2]. "I wonder if[3] this is the key to the secret garden," she thought.

And then, a strange thing happened. To Mary it was almost like magic. A gust[4] of wind blew[5] aside[6] some ivy[7] from the wall. On the wall, Mary could clearly see the round knob[8] of a door. Below the knob was a keyhole[9].

Mary knew, then, that this was the door to the secret garden. What else could it be?

1. **excited** [ɪkˋsaɪtɪd] (a.) 興奮的
2. **all of a sudden** 突然地
3. **wonder if** 想知道是否……
4. **gust** [gʌst] (n.) 一陣強風
5. **blow** [bloʊ] (v.) 吹；刮
   (blow-blew-blown)
6. **aside** [əˋsaɪd] (adv.) 到旁邊
7. **ivy** [ˋaɪvi] (n.) 常春藤
8. **knob** [nɑ:b] (n.) 球型把手
9. **keyhole** [ˋki:hoʊl] (n.) 鑰匙孔

The Secret Garden

Her hands shook[10] so much that she almost couldn't put the key in the keyhole. Mary looked around to make sure that no one was looking. Then, quietly, she slipped[11] through the doorway and closed the door behind her.

"Oh my!" Mary said as she looked around herself. The high walls of the garden were covered with[12] the stems[13] of roses. The rose bushes[14] were scattered[15] throughout[16] the garden and were tangled[17] together. "I must be in heaven[18]," she said.

11. **shake** [ʃeɪk] (v.) 搖動
   (shake-shook-shaken)
12. **slip** [slɪp] (v.) 滑動；滑行
13. **be covered with** 覆蓋著某物
14. **stem** [stem] (n.) 莖
15. **bush** [buʃ] (n.) 灌木；矮樹叢
16. **scatter** [ˋskætər] (v.) 使分散
17. **throughout** [θruːˋaʊt] (prep.)
   遍及；遍佈
18. **tangle** [ˋtæŋɡəl] (v.)
   使糾結；使糾纏
19. **heaven** [ˋhevən] (n.) 天堂

One Point Lesson

● I wonder if this is the key to the secret garden.
   我想要知道這是不是秘密花園的鑰匙。

if：是否（if 子句可以像 whether 一樣，引介間接問句。）

e.g. I asked him **if** he would go. 我問他是否會去。

37

On the ground, the grass was brown. There were the stems of wild flowers everywhere. But Mary couldn't see any buds[1] either.

The garden was a beautiful place, but there didn't seem to be much life[2]. Perhaps it was wonderful because it was Mary's own place. Nobody else knew about it, except for[3] Mr. Craven. And he never went there, anyway[4].

Mary looked closely[5] at a flower bed. She pulled away[6] some leaves, dead grass and weeds[7] from the ground. When she put her nose right[8] to the ground, she could see a few little, pale[9] green points[10] sticking[11] out of the ground.

"This garden isn't quite dead, yet," she said.

1. **bud** [bʌd] (n.) 芽；葉芽
2. **life** [laɪf] (n.) 生命
3. **except for** 除了……以外
4. **anyway** [`enɪweɪ] (adv.)
   而且；再說
5. **closely** [`klousli] (adv.)
   仔細地；近地
6. **pull away** 扯掉
7. **weed** [wiːd] (n.) 雜草
8. **right** [raɪt] (adv.) 恰好地
9. **pale** [peɪl] (a.) 蒼白的；淡的
10. **point** [pɔɪnt] (n.) 尖端；尖頭
11. **stick** [stɪk] (v.) 伸出
    (stick-stuck-stuck)

🎧 12 Mary went home that evening happily. She had found her secret place in the world. She decided to make that garden come back to life.

At dinnertime, Mary suddenly said, "I need a shovel[1]."

"What do you need a shovel for[2]?" Martha asked.

Mary knew that she had to keep[3] her secret place.

"Well, this is such a[4] lovely[5] place. I thought that if I had a little shovel and some seed[6] I could make a little garden."

"Well, that's a wonderful idea! Why don't you[7] write a letter to my little brother, Dickon. He knows all the best places to buy that stuff[8]. He's always gardening[9]."

1. **shovel** [ˈʃʌvəl] (n.) 鏟子
2. **what . . . for?** 為什麼？
   =why?
3. **keep** [kiːp] (v.) 保護
4. **such a** 這麼……；如此……
5. **lovely** [ˈlʌvli] (a.) 可愛的
6. **seed** [siːd] (n.) 種子
7. **why don't you . . . ?**
   你為什麼不……？
8. **stuff** [stʌf] (n.) 東西；材料
9. **garden** [ˈgɑːrdn] (v.)
   做園藝工作
10. **wrap up** 包裹
11. **envelope** [ˈenvəloup] (n.) 信封

After dinner, Mary wrote a letter to Dickon.
She wrapped some money up [10] with the letter and
put it in the envelope [11].

"Oh, I can't wait!" Mary said excitedly.

One Point Lesson

● I thought that **if I had** a little shovel and some seed **I could make** a little garden. 我想假如我有小鏟子和一些種子的話，我就可以建造一座小花園。

假設語氣：<u>If + 主詞 + 動詞過去式，主詞 + should/would/could/might + 動詞</u>。（if 子句中 I, he, she, it 後面的 be 動詞，可用 was 或 were。were 在正式和非正式文章中都很常見，同時美式英語中都固定使用 were。）

e.g. **If I were** a bird, **I could fly** to you.
假如我是一隻鳥，我會飛向你。

The Secret Garden

It had been almost a month since Mary had come to the manor. She was becoming fatter, healthier and happier than she had ever been.

The next morning, Mary learned[1] that Mr. Craven had gone to Austria for a trip. Besides[2] a couple of[3] servants and Mary, there would be no one left[4] in the house.

"No one will disturb[5] me now," she thought. "I can work in the garden as I please[6]."

When she walked down the path to the garden early that morning, she heard a strange whistling[7] sound.

Mary saw a boy sitting in a tree. On his shoulder was a squirrel[8]. Around him were several robins and rabbits sitting on their hind legs[9]. The animals all seemed to[10] be listening to the boy's song.

1. **learn** [lɜːrn] (v.) 得知
2. **besides** [bɪˋsaɪdz] (prep.) 除……之外
3. **a couple of** 一些
4. **left** [left] (a.) 被留下的
5. **disturb** [dɪˋstɜːrb] (v.) 妨礙；打擾
6. **please** [pliːz] (v.) 使喜歡；使高興
7. **whistling** [ˋwɪsəlɪŋ] (a.) 發出哨聲的
8. **squirrel** [ˋskwɜːrəl] (n.) 松鼠
9. **hind legs** 後腿
10. **seem to** 似乎

"Don't come any closer," the boy said. "You'll scare the animals away[1]." Mary stopped walking[2].

"Hi. I'm Dickon," he said. "And you must be Mary. Pleased to meet you. I've brought the garden tools[3] and the seeds you were asking for[4]." He spoke to her as if[5] he knew her quite well.

"Thanks, Dickon," said Mary. "I'm very happy to meet you, too. How come[6] you have so many animal friends?"

"Why, because I'm an animal myself. Come on, Mary. Let's start gardening. Where's your garden?"

Mary knew then that she couldn't keep her garden to herself forever[7].

"Dickon," Mary said. "Can you keep a secret?"

"I always keep secrets," he said.

1. **scare . . . away** 嚇跑……
2. **stop + V-ing** [stɑːp] (v.) 停止 (做某件事)
3. **tool** [tuːl] (n.) 工具
4. **ask for** 要求
5. **as if** 好似
6. **How come . . . ?** 怎麼會
7. **forever** [fərˋevər] (adv.) 永遠
8. **steal** [stiːl] (v.) 偷竊 (steal-stole-stolen)
9. **mean** [miːn] (v.) 意指；意謂
10. **lock up** 鎖起來；關起來
11. **in years** 數年來
12. **bring back to life** 起死回生
13. **lead** [liːd] (v.) 領路；引導 (lead-led-led)

"Don't tell anybody. I've stolen[8] a garden."

"What do you mean[9] you've 'stolen a garden'?"

"Well, there's this garden that has been locked up[10] for many years. Mr. Craven said that nobody could go into the garden. I found that garden myself. It's dying because nobody has taken care of it in years[11]."

"Alright, Mary. Show me the garden. If there's anybody who can bring it back[12] to life, I can."

Mary then led[13] Dickon to the secret garden.

One Point Lesson

● He spoke to her **as if** he knew her quite well.
他和她說話的樣子,似乎和她很熟。

as if 和 **as though** 可以用來比喻事情「就像⋯⋯一樣」,雖然事實不可能如此。

● She talk **as if** (= **as though**) she were a princess.
她說話的樣子好像她是公主一樣。

Dickon looked around and around. He was just as amazed[1] as Mary was to see the garden.

"It is a strange, pretty place!"

They worked all day long[2] that sunny day. They weeded[3] and raked[4] leaves. They planted[5] seeds and pulled out[6] dead flowers. They watered[7] plants and made flower beds.

"There's a lot more work to do here!" Dickon said, seeing all that they had done.

"Will you come again and help me?" Mary asked.

1. **amazed** [əˈmeɪzd] (a.) 吃驚的
2. **all day long** 一整天
3. **weed** [wiːd] (v.) 除去雜草
4. **rake** [reɪk] (v.) 耙平
5. **plant** [plænt] (v.) 栽種
6. **pull out** 拔出
7. **water** [ˈwɒːtər] (v.) 給……澆水
8. **shut** [ʃʌt] (v.) 關閉
9. **waken up** 喚醒；弄醒
10. **feel like** 感到好似
11. **no longer** 不再是
12. **full off** 充滿……

"I'll come every day if you want me to," he
answered, with a big smile on his face. "It's the
best fun I ever had in my life—shut[8] in here
and wakening up[9] a garden."

At the end of the long day, as Mary lay in bed,
she felt like[10] she had begun a new life. England
was no longer[11] a lonely place. It was a place
full of[12] animals, friends, flowers and a secret
garden. Who could want anything more?

One Point Lesson

"I'll come every day if you want me to," he answered, with a
big smile on his face.
他掛著燦爛笑容，答道：「假如你要我來，我每天都會來。」

with: 帶著……的；有……的
with + 名詞：介系詞片語，可以當做副詞來修飾動詞，所以介系詞
片語也稱做副詞片語。

e.g. "I lost my purse." Martha said, with a sad look.
瑪莎帶著難過的表情說：「我的錢包掉了。」

A True or False.

1 Dicken had a lot of animal friends. ☐T ☐F

2 Dicken was Martha's father. ☐T ☐F

3 Dicken didn't know where to buy garden tools. ☐T ☐F

4 Dicken never kept secrets. ☐T ☐F

5 Dicken was very good at gardening. ☐T ☐F

B Fill in the blanks with the given words.

> blooming   determined   tangled
> taken   amazed

1 The rose bushes were _____ together.

2 The roses weren't _____ yet.

3 She was _____ to bring her secret place back to life.

4 Mary was _____ that Dickon had so many animal friends.

5 The garden was dying because nobody had _____ care of it in years.

C Complete the sentences with this sentence pattern "was/were+-ing".

> Mary *walked* toward the bird.
> ⇨ Mary *was walking* toward the bird.

1 The bird stood on a small mound of earth.

⇨ _____

2 A gust of wind blew aside some ivy from the wall.

⇨ _____

3 Her hand shook so much that she almost couldn't put the key in the keyhole.

⇨ _____

D Rearrange the sentences in chronological order.

1 Mary pulled a ring out of a hole that had a key on it.

2 Mary unlocked the door with the key.

3 Mary said, "I must be in heaven."

4 The robin tried to get Mary's attention.

5 Mary could see a door on the wall.

_____ ⇨ _____ ⇨ _____ ⇨ _____ ⇨ _____

Chapter Three

The Little Craven, Colin

That night, Mary was woken up by the crying sound again.

"That isn't the wind," she said. "I know it isn't. I'm going to find out where that crying is coming from."

Mary got up[1] and walked down a long, dark corridor[2]. The sound was becoming louder[3]. Suddenly, she saw a glimmer[4] of light coming from beneath[5] a door.

Someone was crying in the room beyond[6] the door. It sounded like[7] a young boy.

Mary opened the door. In the room, Mary saw a boy lying on a bed, crying. The boy looked very thin and white. He looked sick.

---

1. **get up** 起床
2. **corridor** [`kɔːrɪdər] (n.) 迴廊
3. **louder** [laʊdər] (a.) (loud 的比較級) 較大聲的
4. **glimmer** [`glɪmər] (n.) 微光
5. **beneath** [bɪ`niːθ] (prep.) 在⋯⋯之下
6. **beyond** [bɪ`jɒnd] (prep.) 越過
7. **sound like** 聽起來像
8. **scream** [skriːm] (v.) 尖叫

When the boy saw Mary, he screamed[8].
"A ghost[9]! A ghost! Help!"

"Be quiet," Mary whispered[10]. "Do I look like a
ghost to you?"

"I suppose[11] not. Who are you, then?"

"My name's Mary Lennox. Who are you?"

Mary stared at[12] his eyes. They were gray[13] and
looked too big for his face.

"I'm Colin Craven. I'm Archibald Craven's son."

9. **ghost** [goʊst] (n.) 鬼；幽靈
10. **whisper** [ˋwɪspər] (v.) 低語
11. **suppose** [səˋpoʊz] (v.) 猜想
12. **stare at** 凝視著
13. **gray** [greɪ] (a.) 灰色的

Mary clapped[1] her hands with delight[2]. "That's wonderful. That means that you're my little cousin[3]. Mr. Craven is my uncle. But why didn't you go to Austria with your father?"

"I never go anywhere[4] with him. In fact[5], I haven't even seen him for a long time. He doesn't like to look at me because I remind him of my mother[6]. She died when I was a baby. So I spend most of my time alone[7].

My doctor said I'm not supposed to meet people. He's worried[8] that I might[9] catch[10] the flu[11] from them. If I live, I may be a hunchback[12] like my father. But I'm too sick to live."

"My mother died, too," said Mary. "So did my father. That's why I'm living here."

1. **clap** [klæp] (v.) 鼓掌
2. **delight** [dɪˋlaɪt] (n.) 欣喜
3. **cousin** [ˋkʌzən] (n.) 堂 (或表) 兄弟姐妹
4. **anywhere** [ˋeniwer] (n.) 任何地方
5. **in fact** 事實上
6. **remind A of B** 提醒 A 想起 B
7. **alone** [əˋloʊn] (adv.) 單獨地
8. **worried** [ˋwɜːrid] (a.) 擔心的
9. **might** [maɪt] (aux.) 可能
10. **catch** [kætʃ] (v.) 染上 (疾病) (catch-caught-caught)
11. **flu** [fluː] (n.) 流行性感冒
12. **hunchback** [ˋhʌntʃbæk] (n.) 駝背者
13. **realize** [ˋrɪəlaɪz] (v.) 領悟

"That's strange. How come I haven't seen you around here?" Colin asked.

"Oh, I spend most of my time in my garden." Mary realized[13] then that she had said something she shouldn't have said.

One Point Lesson

♦ Mary realized then that she had said something **she shouldn't have said.** 瑪麗知道她說了不該說的話。

---

should not have + 過去分詞：不應該……（描述一件已經完成，但不應該做的事。）

e.g. You **shouldn't have yelled** out. 你不應該大喊大叫。

"What garden?" Colin asked.

"Oh, it's just a . . . a garden nearby[1]."

"Which one?"

Mary didn't want to say too much for she was afraid[2] Colin would tell others about the garden. But Mary felt bad about lying[3] to her cousin. He was so much like herself.

"Colin, can you keep a secret?" she asked.

"I guess[4] so. I don't know. I've never had a secret before. Okay. If you tell me your secret, I promise[5] I won't tell anybody about it."

"There's a secret garden nearby," Mary said. "Your father didn't want anyone to go in there. So, he locked the door to the garden and buried the key. But I found the key. Now, a boy named 'Dickon' and I are trying to bring the garden back to life."

1. **nearby** [ˋnɪr͵baɪ] (adv.) 在附近
2. **afraid** [əˋfreɪd] (a.) 害怕的
3. **lie** [laɪ] (v.) 撒謊
4. **guess** [gɛs] (v.) 猜測
5. **promise** [ˋprɑːmɪs] (v.) 承諾
6. **grow** [groʊ] (v.) 變得 (grow-grew-grown)
7. **wide** [waɪd] (a.) 寬的
8. **mysterious** [mɪˋstɪrɪəs] (a.) 神秘的

The Secret Garden

As Mary spoke about the secret garden, Colin's eyes grew[6] wide[7]. He had never heard about such an exciting and mysterious[8] place.

19

"Mary, could you take[1] me to the garden?" Colin asked. "I really want to go. If only someone could push[2] my wheelchair[3] out there."

"You're not supposed to leave the house."

"But since my father is gone, I'm in charge[4] here. The servants have to listen to[5] everything I say."

"I don't know, Colin. I think Mrs. Medlock will be very angry if you go outside."

Colin had a very sad look on his face.

"If you get better[6], Colin, then maybe I can take you outside."

"Alright[7], I will," Colin said, happily. "I'll get better. Then take me outside[8] to the garden. Please, Mary. Please do that for me."

1. **take** [teɪk] (v.) 帶
   (take-took-taken)
2. **push** [pʊʃ] (v.) 推
3. **wheelchair** [`wiːltʃer] (n.)
   輪椅
4. **be in charge** 負責掌管
5. **listen to** 聽從
6. **get better** 變得較好
7. **alright** [ˌɒlˋraɪt] (adv.)
   沒問題地
8. **outside** [`autˋsaɪd] (n.) 外面
9. **late** [leɪt] (adv.) 晚
10. **the most** 最多
11. **kind** [kaɪnd] (n.) 種類
12. **on and on** 繼續不停地

Mary and Colin talked late[9] into the evening.
They spoke about many things. Mary told Colin
how life had been in India. And Colin told her how
he felt being in a dark room with only books.

But the thing that they spoke the most[10]
about was the garden. He wanted to know where
it was, what kind[11] of flowers there were, and how
big it was. On and on[12], Colin asked question
after question. The boy felt happier that evening
than he had in a long time.

20

It rained heavily[1] the next day. Since[2] Mary couldn't go out in the rain, she was with Colin for the whole[3] day. When Martha found Mary in Colin's room, she got angry[4].

"It's okay," Colin said. "She has my permission[5] to stay[6] here." The servants couldn't say 'no' to Colin.

When Colin's doctor came, he was very upset, as well.

"What if this girl gives you the flu?"

"She won't. Besides, I feel healthier when she's around," said Colin. The doctor saw that this was true. Colin looked healthier than he had.

The rain continued[7] for a week, and Mary spent the week with Colin. There was the constant[8] sound of laughter[9] from his room. Every day, Colin seemed to[10] get stronger and stronger. He really wanted to go to the garden.

1. **heavily** [`hevɪli] (a.) 猛烈地
2. **since** [sɪns] (conj.) 自從
3. **whole** [houl] (a.) 全部的
4. **get angry** 生氣
5. **permission** [pər`mɪʃən] (n.) 允許；許可
6. **stay** [steɪ] (v.) 停留
7. **continue** [kən`tɪnjuː] (v.) 繼續
8. **constant** [`kɑːnstənt] (a.) 持續的；不斷的
9. **laughter** [`læftər] (n.) 笑聲
10. **seem to** 似乎

Every day, Colin seemed to get stronger and stronger.
柯林的身體似乎日益強健。

---

get + 形容詞：get 可當連綴動詞，後接形容詞，表示「變成」。
get + 形容詞的比較級 + and + 形容詞的比較級：變得愈來愈……

e.g It **gets warmer and warmer** when spring comes.
春天來臨時，天氣愈來愈暖和。
I **got healthy.**
我變得健康。

On the first clear[1] morning, Mary woke up very early. She opened the window and smelled fresh air. As soon as she put on[2] her clothes, Mary ran to the garden. Dickon was already hard at[3] work.

"Look!" Dickon said. "The garden is alive[4]!"
Mary looked around. It was true! Green points were pushing through[5] the earth everywhere. Leaf buds[6] were growing on the rose bushes. Flowers were blooming orange, purple, yellow and red. Best of all[7], the robin was building[8] a nest[9].

"When did this happen?" Mary asked, amazed.
"Over[10] the last week. The rain did the garden some good[11]."
Mary was happy to see such life in something that she believed was dead.

1. **clear** [klɪr] (a.) 明亮的
2. **put on** 穿上；戴上
3. **be hard at** 努力做……
4. **alive** [ə`laɪv] (a.) 有生氣的
5. **push through** 擠著；穿過
6. **bud** [bʌd] (n.) 芽
7. **best of all** 最棒的是
8. **build** [bɪld] (v.) 建造
9. **nest** [nest] (n.) 窩；巢
10. **over** [`ouvər] (prep.) 在某期間
11. **do good** 使有益處
12. **exactly** [ɪg`zæktli] (adv.) 確切地；完全地
13. **enough** [ɪ`nʌf] (adv.) 足夠地；充分地

As Mary worked with Dickon that morning, she told him about Colin. Dickon had already known about him from Martha.

"People say Mr. Craven can't see him when he is awake, because his eyes look exactly[12] like his mother's."

"I feel sorry for Colin. And he really wants to visit the garden. He can't because he's so sick."

"That's too bad," said Dickon. "We must bring him outside with us. I can push his wheelchair easily enough[13]."

One Point Lesson

- The rain **did the garden some good.**
  雨水滋潤了花園。

do + 名詞 + good：對⋯⋯有好處；對⋯⋯有益

e.g. The medicine will **do you good.** 藥對你有益處。

When Mary went to see Colin after dinner, Colin was very sad. He had spent a beautiful spring day inside, all alone. He looked as bad as he had looked the first time Mary saw him.

"Mary," Colin said, "I think I'm going to die. I'll never see your garden."

"Nonsense," Mary said. "You just feel bad[1] because you stay inside all the time. You never breathe[2] the fresh air. You never use your muscles[3]. You need to[4] go outside."

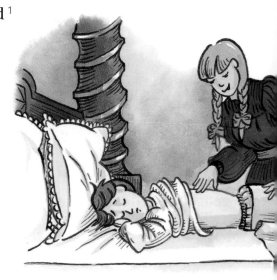

1. **feel bad** 感到難過
2. **breathe** [briːð] (v.) 呼吸
3. **muscle** [ˋmʌsəl] (n.) 肌肉
4. **need to** 需要去⋯⋯
5. **hump** [hʌmp] (n.) 背部隆肉
6. **back** [bæk] (n.) 背部
7. **feel** [fiːl] (v.) 感覺
8. **nothing** [ˋnʌθɪŋ] (n.) 無物
9. **imagine** [ɪˋmædʒɪn] (v.) 想像
10. **budding** [ˋbʌdɪŋ] (a.) 萌芽的

"No, Mary," he said. "I can't! I'm growing a hump[5] on my back[6]. I can feel[7] it. Look!"

Mary looked at his back.

"There's nothing[8] there, Colin. You're imagining[9] everything. You have to come work in our garden. The sooner, the better."

"Alright, Mary," he said. "I'll come with you as soon as I can."

Then, Mary told Colin about the budding[10] leaves and the blooming flowers.

That night Colin dreamed about the earth and the flowers, the animals and the plants. He dreamed about the secret garden.

One Point Lesson

The sooner, the better. 愈快愈好。

the + 形容詞或副詞比較級，the + 形容詞或副詞比較級：愈……，愈……

e.g. The more book you read, the more information you can get.
你讀愈多書，就會獲得愈多資訊。

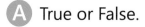 A True or False.

1 Colin was very healthy.   T F

2 Colin hadn't seen his father in many years.   T F

3 Colin was afraid of ghosts.   T F

4 Colin was Mary's cousin.   T F

5 Colin had never had a secret before he met Mary.   T F

6 Colin never cried.   T F

B Match.

1 Colin needed   •

2 Colin's doctor said   •

3 Colin felt happier that evening   •

4 Colin promised   •

5 A young boy   •

A than he had felt in a someone long time.

B was crying in the room.

C that he would get better.

D that he's not supposed to meet anyone.

E to push his wheelchair outside.

C Choose the correct answer.

1 Why did Mary spend a whole week inside talking to Colin?

(a) Because she had a lot to say.

(b) Because she had to take care of Colin.

(c) Because it rained heavily every day.

2 How come Mr. Craven doesn't like to look at his son?

(a) Because Colin reminds him of his wife.

(b) Because Colin had a hump on his back.

(c) Because Mr. Craven had the flu.

D Correct the sentences by changing one word.

1 Dickon is Martha's cousin.

⇨ _____

2 Mary was awakened by the sound of talking.

⇨ _____

3 Mr. Craven opened the garden and buried the key.

⇨ _____

English Gardens

Mary came to love flowers and gardens when she went to live at Misselthwaite Manor. Many English people like gardens very much. They enjoy growing plants and flowers in their own gardens and they also like to visit the gardens of big houses like Misselthwaite Manor.

The gardens of Misselthwaite Manor reflect different English gardening styles. When Mary passed through some gardens to get to the Secret Garden, she found them all well-cared for.

The lawns of these gardens were favorite places for the English to play games such as tennis or bowling. There are also orchard gardens, where all sorts of fruit trees like apple and pear grow. In addition, many English countryside mansions had kitchen gardens, where vegetables were grown for food.

The Secret Garden represents the trend in 18th century English gardening. English gardeners tried to adopt a more natural look to the gardens to show nature at its best. This is the type of garden that Mary Lennox falls in love with and finds so precious.

Chapter Four

I'll Live Forever

The next morning, Mary went to Colin's room and said, "I'm going to see Dickon, but I'll come back[1]."

In five minutes, she was with Dickon in the garden. When Mary and Dickon started working, she told him about what Colin had said the night before.

"In the springtime[2], everyone should be outside working," Dickon said.

"Folks[3] need to be listening to the birds and digging[4] in the dirt[5]. If people aren't doing that, then they aren't living. We need to bring him out with us soon. Then he'll get better."

"I have an idea," said Mary. "Since he can't come out here, why don't we bring the garden to him."

1. **come back** 回來
2. **springtime** [`sprɪŋtaɪm] (n.) 春天
3. **folks** [foʊks] (n.) 人們
4. **dig** [dɪg] (v.) 挖掘 (dig-dug-dug)
5. **dirt** [dɝt] (n.) 泥；土

> One Point Lesson

• **Since** he can't come out here, why don't we bring the garden to him.
既然他不能出去，我們可以把花園帶來給他。

since：自從……以來；既然；因為

I have known her **since** she was a baby.
從她還是嬰兒時，我就認識她了。
Since we are not very busy, we can take a rest.
既然我們沒有很多事要做，就可以休息一下。

24

Dickon was confused[1]. "What do you mean?"

"I mean, let's bring him some of the animals and the plants from the garden."

"That sounds like a wonderful idea."

It seemed as if a magician[2] visited the garden every day and night.

When Mary went back and sat down close to Colin's bed, he began to sniff[3].

"What's the smell?" he asked.

"It's the wind from the garden." replied Mary.

The next morning, Mary burst into[4] Colin's room.

"Spring has come," she yelled out[5]. "Let's open the windows, Colin."

Mary opened all of the windows in the room. The room was filled with[6] the sounds of birds singing. A fresh breeze[7] came in the window. She placed[8] two potted[9] roses on the windowsill[10].

---

1. **confused** [kənˋfjuːzd] (a.) 困惑的；惶恐的
2. **magician** [məˋdʒɪʃən] (n.) 魔術師
3. **sniff** [snɪf] (v.) 嗅；聞
4. **burst into** 突然衝進 (burst-burst-burst)
5. **yell out** 大聲地叫出
6. **be filled with** 被⋯⋯充滿
7. **breeze** [briːz] (n.) 微風；和風
8. **place** [pleɪs] (v.) 放置
9. **potted** [pɑːtɪd] (a.) 盆栽的
10. **windowsill** 窗臺

"It's time that you stopped thinking about death and humps on your back. It's time to think about being healthy. Come in, Dickon."

Dickon walked in the room. "Hello, Colin," he said.

25

Colin was amazed[1] at what he saw. He almost jumped out of[2] bed with excitement[3].

Dickon had robins on both[4] shoulders and he was carrying[5] a baby lamb in his arms. A little red fox also walked by his side. As Dickon placed the lamb on the floor, two squirrels ran in the door. They jumped on Colin's bed and the boy cried for joy[6].

Colin decided at that moment that he would go outside that day.

"I need someone to push my wheelchair," he said.

1. **amazed** [əˋmeɪzd] (a.) 吃驚的；驚奇的
2. **jump out of** 自……跳出
3. **excitement** [ɪkˋsaɪtmənt] (n.) 興奮；激動
4. **both** [bouθ] (a.) 兩者都

"I can do that," Dickon said. "You don't need to worry about falling[7], either[8]."

Colin then called Mrs. Medlock.

"Please tell all of the servants that I'm going outside today," he told her. "And I may go out every day from now on[9] if the weather is nice. When I go outside, I don't want any servants to follow[10] me. Mary and Dickon will take care of me. You don't have to worry about anything."

"Yes, Colin," Mrs. Medlock said.

5. **carry** [ˋkæri] (v.) 抱
6. **for joy** 由於欣喜
7. **falling** [fɔːlɪŋ] (n.) 落下；跌倒
8. **either** [ˋaɪðə] (adv.) 也不
9. **from now on** 從現在開始
10. **follow** [ˋfɑːlou] (v.) 跟隨

26

Then Colin did something that surprised everyone. He threw[1] the blankets[2] off of[3] himself and placed his feet on the floor. Very slowly, he stood up. His legs shook a lot. He took five short steps[4] and sat in the wheelchair. As he sat down, Colin was dripping with[5] sweat[6].

"I haven't stood up in two years," he said.

Dickon pushed Colin to the staircase[7]. Then he helped him to walk down the stairs[8] and outside. Colin sat down again in his wheelchair all by himself[9].

As Colin was pushed along the pathway[10], tears of joy fell down[11] his face.

1. **throw off** 扔掉
2. **blanket** [ˋblæŋkɪt] (n.) 毛毯;毯子
3. **of** [əv] (prep.) ……的;屬於……
4. **take a step** 跨出一步
5. **drip with** 滴下……
6. **sweat** [swet] (n.) 汗水
7. **staircase** [ˋsterkeɪs] (n.) 樓梯
8. **stairs** [sterz] (n.) 樓梯
9. **by oneself** 單獨地
10. **pathway** [ˋpæθweɪ] (n.) 路;小徑
11. **fall down** 落下
12. **at last** 最終;最後
13. **gate** 大門;柵欄門
14. **whisper** [ˋwɪspər] (v.) 低語;私語
15. **gasp** [gæsp] (v.) 倒抽一口氣

When at last[12] they got to the gate[13] of the secret garden, the children began to whisper[14].

"Okay, Colin," Mary whispered.

"You can't tell anyone about this place."

"Quick! Quick! Push me in!" Colin said. "Somebody may see us!"

As Colin was pushed into the secret garden, he gasped[15]. The whole garden was alive with colors, sounds and smells.

One Point Lesson

Colin sat down again in his wheelchair all by himself.
柯林又再度靠自己坐在輪椅裡。

人身代名詞 - self：反身代名詞。

He killed himself.（他自己）他自殺了。

I did it myself.（我親自）我自己做的。

oneself 片語用法

by oneself 單獨地；親自地   for oneself 為自己
beside oneself 忘形   of oneself 自行

27

The flower beds and rose bushes looked like they were painted[1] violet[2], blue, yellow and red. The roses formed[3] bridges above their heads. Bees[4] buzzed[5] through the flowers and birds sang in the trees.

Colin had spent hours imagining what the garden would be like. But he never imagined it was as beautiful as this.

As the sun fell upon[6] Colin's face, Mary noticed[7] that he looked different. He had a glow[8] of color in his cheeks and his eyes sparkled[9].

1. **paint** [peɪnt] (v.) 塗以顏色
2. **violet** [ˋvaɪəlɪt] (a.) 紫色的
3. **form** [fɔːrm] (v.) 形成；構成
4. **bee** [biː] (n.) 蜜蜂
5. **buzz** [bʌz] (v.) 嗡嗡叫
6. **fall upon** 落在……

"I'll get well!" he cried out. "I'll get well! And I'll live forever! I've seen the spring. Now I'm going to see the summer. I'm going to see everything grow here. I'm going to grow here, too."

That day, Colin got out of[10] his chair and walked around a little. And when he came back the next day, he walked a little more. Soon, he was strong enough to work in the garden.

7. **notice** [`noutɪs] (v.) 注意到
8. **glow** [ɡlou] (n.) 光輝
9. **sparkle** [`spɑːrkəl] (v.) 閃耀出火花
10. **get out of** 從……出來

28

As the weeks passed[1], Colin worked hard in the garden. Some days, however, he preferred[2] to sit back[3] and watch everything grow.

One day, as the children lay in the sweet-smelling[4] grass, Mary asked Colin something she'd wanted to ask him for a long time.

"What are you going to tell your father when he comes home?"

"I won't tell him anything. I'm just going to walk up to[5] him and show him how healthy I am."

Colin was as healthy and strong as anybody of his age[6].

In addition[7] to the work that Colin did in the garden, he started exercising[8] every day. Soon, he became strong. He seemed to be growing, as well.

1. **pass** [pæs] (v.) 經過
2. **prefer** [prɪˋfɜːr] (v.) 寧可;更喜歡
3. **sit back** 坐下來休息
4. **sweet-smelling** 芳香的
5. **walk up to** 起身走向⋯⋯
6. **age** [eɪdʒ] (n.) 年齡
7. **in addition** 除了
8. **exercise** [ˋeksəsaɪz] (v.) 運動

29

One day, Colin dropped[1] his shovel and said, "Mary! Dickon! Look at me!" Colin stood up very straight[2]. "Do you remember the first day you brought me here?"

"Of course," Dickon replied.

"All at once[3], I remember what I looked like that day. It seems strange. I was so sick then. But I'm so healthy now! Can it be true? Am I really well?"

"Yes. You are, Colin," Mary said.

"I am. I know it now. I really will live forever. I wish my father would come home. I want him to see me now. And I wish my mother were alive, too. I wish she could see what a strong young boy I am."

"I think your mother is alive," said Dickon.

"I think she's alive in this very[4] garden. She's growing[5] in the flowers and in the trees. She's growing in the grass and the bushes. And she's growing in you, too, Colin."

---

1. **drop** [drɑːp] (v.) 丟下
2. **straight** [streɪt] (adv.) 挺直地
3. **all at once** 突然
4. **very** [ˋverɪ] (a.) 正是
5. **grow** [groʊ] (v.) (有形或無形的) 生長

One Point Lesson

● **Can it be true?** 這會是真的嗎？

can：可能；可能會

can 用在否定句、疑問句，或是和具否定意味的字連用時，表示懷疑或猜測某件事的可能。

e.g **It cannot be true.** 這不可能是真的。

A True or False.

1 Colin hadn't walked for two years.　　T　F

2 Dickon didn't want to bring Colin outside.　　T　F

3 Dickon brought animals into Colin's room.　　T　F

4 Colin imagined that the secret garden was more beautiful than it really was.　　T　F

5 Mary brought two potted roses into Colin's room.　　T　F

B Fill in the blanks with the given words.

shook　buzzed　healthy　alive　sang　busily

1 The whole garden was _____ with colors, sounds and smells.

2 Honeybees flew around the children working _____.

3 When Colin stood up, his legs _____ a lot.

4 Bees _____ in the flowers and birds _____ in the trees.

5 Colin became very _____.

C Choose the correct answer.

1 What did Dickon think would help Colin?

(a) To get him out into the garden.

(b) To see his father.

(c) To see another doctor.

2 How did Mary and Dickon take Colin to the secret garden?

(a) They helped him to walk.

(b) They carried him.

(c) They took him in his wheelchair.

D Rearrange the sentences in chronological order.

1 Dickon brought his animal friends into Colin's room.

2 Dickon pushed Colin's wheelchair to the secret garden.

3 Colin started working in the garden.

4 Mary ran into Colin's room and put two potted roses on the windowsill.

5 Colin stood up for the first time in two years.

_____ ⇨ _____ ⇨ _____ ⇨ _____ ⇨ _____

Chapter Five

🎧 ³⁰ It's Me, Father

That spring, the secret garden came alive¹.
The children came alive with it.

There was a man, however, who hadn't felt
alive in a long time. He had traveled around the
world for ten years. But he never felt anything
but² sadness³ and boredom⁴.

He was a tall man with crooked shoulders and
an unhappy face. His name was Archibald Craven.

1. **come alive** 恢復生氣
2. **but** [bət] (prep.) 只有
3. **sadness** [`sædnɪs] (n.) 悲傷

4. **boredom** [`bɔːrdəm] (n.)
   無聊；厭倦

He traveled to many beautiful places. But he never stayed anywhere[1] for more than a few days. He was so sad that he never noticed the beautiful things around him.

One day a strange thing happened[2]. He was in a beautiful valley[3] in Austria. The valley was very quiet. He had walked a long way alone. He began to feel tired and lay down[4] by a stream[5] to take a nap[6].

When he fell asleep[7], he began to[8] dream.

1. **anywhere** [`eniwer] (n.) 任何地方
2. **happen** [`hæpən] (v.) 偶然發生
3. **valley** [`væli] (n.) 山谷
4. **lie down** 躺下
5. **stream** [stri:m] (n.) 河流
6. **take a nap** 打個盹兒
7. **fall asleep** 睡著
8. **begin to** 開始

His dream was so real,
however, that he didn't think
he was dreaming.
He thought he heard
someone calling him.
The voice was far away[9].

"Archie!" he heard. And then again, he heard the voice clearer[10] than before. "Archie!"

"Lillias! Lillias! Is that you?" Lillias was Archibald Craven's dead wife. "Lillias! Where are you?"

The voice came back like a beautiful song. "I'm in the garden."

Then, the dream ended.

When he woke up[11], he felt very calm[12] and happy. He thought about the dream carefully.

"In the garden!" he said to himself. "But the door is locked. And the key is buried."

9. **far away** 遙遠的
10. **clear** [klɪr] (a.) 清楚的
11. **wake up** 醒來
12. **calm** [kɑːm] (a.) 平靜的

🎧 32

Archibald looked at the stream. He saw birds come and dip[1] their heads in it. After taking a drink[2], they flew away[3].

He looked carefully at a bunch[4] of wild flowers. The leaves of the flowers were wet from the splashing[5] stream. The flowers were deep blue[6]. The color reminded him of the lake next to Misselthwaite Manor.

Archibald found himself looking at them as he had looked at such things years ago.

"I will go back home," he said.

On the long train ride[7] back to his home, Archibald thought about his son. He realized that he hadn't paid any attention[8] to him for ten years.

In fact, he had only wanted to forget about him. He had not meant to[9] be a bad father. But he had hardly been a father at all. He rarely[10] even saw the boy. He only saw Colin when he was asleep.

"I have been a bad father," Archibald said to himself. "Maybe I can change. Maybe I can be a good father to him from now on."

1. **dip** [dɪp] (v.) 浸泡
   (dip-dipped-dipped)
2. **take a drink** 喝水
3. **fly away** 飛走
   (fly-flew-flown)
4. **bunch** [bʌntʃ] (n.) 束
5. **splashing** [splæʃŋ] (a.) 濺起的
6. **deep blue** 深藍色的
7. **ride** [raɪd] (n.) 搭乘
8. **pay attention** 專心注意
9. **mean to** 有意
11. **rarely** [ˋrerli] (adv.) 很少地

One Point Lesson

◆ But he had **hardly** been a father at all.
但他幾乎一點都不算是父親。

◆ He **rarely** even saw the boy. 他甚至很少去看男孩。

hardly / rarely：幾乎不；很少。與 seldom、scarcely 等否定詞的用法相同，用來修飾動詞時，要放在中位，也就是動詞前，助動詞、情態動詞、be 動詞後。

(e.g) I can **hardly** wait. 我等不及了。
I **seldom** think of politics. 我很少想到政治。

33

As the train passed through[1] beautiful valleys of England, Archibald Craven smiled. It had been years since he had smiled. He felt peace[2] and, even more importantly[3], he felt hope. He knew that his life would get better. He knew that he could make a difference[4] in Colin's life.

When Archibald finally arrived back home, he called for[5] Mrs. Medlock.

"How is my son, Mrs. Medlock?"

"You should go see for yourself, Mr. Craven. I think you'll be surprised."

"Where is he, then?"

"He's in the garden. He goes there every day now. No other people are allowed[6] to go near."

Archibald then went to the garden. He walked down the same path that Mary had walked down on her first day at Misselthwaite Manor.

He walked to the garden's door and stopped. He knew where the door was, even though[7] the ivy hid[8] it but he couldn't remember where he had buried the key.

"Where could that key be?" he thought.

1. **pass through** 穿過；通過
2. **peace** [pi:s] (n.) 平靜
3. **importantly** [ɪmˋpɔːrtəntli] (adv.) 重要地；要緊地
4. **make a difference** 改變
5. **call for** 呼喚
6. **allow** [əˋlaʊ] (v.) 允許
7. **even though** 即使；雖然
8. **hide** [haɪd] (v.) 隱藏 (hide-hid-hidden)

One Point Lesson

You should **go see** for yourself, Mr. Craven.
你應該自己去看看，克萊文先生。

go see: go and see 去看（go+ 原型動詞＝ go+and+ 原型動詞）

e.g. It's time to **go see** the doctor. 該是去看醫生的時間了。

34

Just then[1], he heard sounds. The sounds seemed to be coming from[2] the garden. He heard children playing and laughing aloud[3].

"That's strange," he thought. "Nobody has been in that garden for ten years."

Suddenly, Archibald heard a shout[4] of laughter and a boy ran through[5] the doorway. The boy ran right[6] into Archibald's arms.

He was a tall, handsome boy. He was glowing[7] with life. His strange, gray eyes made Mr. Craven gasp for breath. He had never thought of such a meeting.

"Oh! Who are you, little boy?" he asked.

"It's me, father! Don't you recognize[8] your own son, Colin?"

Mr. Craven couldn't believe his eyes. His boy looked strong and healthy. He had color[9] in his cheeks and in his eyes. He seemed happy. He didn't look at all like the Colin Craven that Archibald knew.

"C-Colin? I can't believe it! Is that really you? You look so different!"

"That's because I've grown, father. I stopped dying and I started living. I was brought back to life. Just like this garden. I want to show you something. Come with me, father."

1. **just then** 就在當時
2. **come from** 來自……
3. **aloud** [əˋlaʊd] (adv.) 大聲地
4. **shout** [ʃaʊt] (n.) 呼喊；喊叫
5. **run through** 穿過；通過
   (run-ran-run)
6. **right** [raɪt] (adv.) 不偏不倚地
7. **glow** [gloʊ] (v.) 發光；發熱
8. **recognize** [ˋrekəgnaɪz] (v.) 認出
9. **color** [ˋkʌlər] (n.) 血色；顏色

Colin then led his father into the garden. The garden was alive with color. It looked more beautiful than it had ever looked before. The colors and the smells of the flowers made Mr. Craven very happy.

"I thought this garden would be dead," Archibald said.
"I thought so, too, at first[1]," said Mary.

"Your niece[2], Mary, brought it alive again," said Dickon.

"Dickon and Colin helped as well," Mary said. "A little magic helped, too. And a robin showed me the door."

"And then the garden brought me back to life," said Colin.

Then, they sat under[3] a tree and Colin told his father everything.

"I don't want this garden to be a secret anymore, father," said Colin. "I want it to be open so that everyone can come here. I want other sick boys to come here, as well. They can be brought back to life just like[4] I was."

1. **at first** 起先
2. **niece** [niːs] (n.) 姪女
3. **under** [ˋʌndər] (prep.) 在……下方
4. **just like** 就如同

36

Then, Archibald Craven and his son walked back to the castle. The servants came out and greeted[1] them. They looked at the boy carefully and realized[2] that he was a new person.

Mr. Craven told his servants that the walls of the garden should be torn down[3].

That autumn, the garden changed again. The leaves changed from green to red, yellow, orange and brown. The flowers withered[4], as well.

Sick children came from around Yorkshire to see the garden. They were happy to see the leaves falling. They knew that the garden would come alive again next year. And maybe they would, too.

1. **greet** [griːt] (v.) 問候；迎接
2. **realize** [ˋriəlaɪz] (v.) 領悟；了解
3. **tear town** 拆除；扯下 (tear-tore-torn)
4. **wither** [ˋwɪðər] (v.) 枯萎；凋謝

A The statements below are about Archibald Craven. Circle either True or False.

❶ He neglected Colin when he saw him.   T   F

❷ He never noticed beautiful things around him.   T   F

❸ He had meant to be a bad father.   T   F

❹ He became hopeful after he had his dream.   T   F

❺ He thought that the garden would be alive.   T   F

❻ He traveled a lot.   T   F

B Spelling.

❶ Archibald Craven is Mary's u __ __ __e.

❷ Mrs. Medlock is Mr. Craven's h o __ __ __ k __ __ __ e r.

❸ Dickon is Martha's b r __ __ __ __ __.

❹ Colin is Mary's c __ __ __ __ n.

❺ Martha is Mr. Craven's m __ __ __.

C Rewrite the sentences with this sentence pattern "had+pp."

> He traveled many beautiful places.
> ⇨ *He had traveled many beautiful places.*

1 The voice came back like a beautiful song.

⇨ _____

2 But the door is locked.

⇨ _____

3 He didn't mean to be a bad father.

⇨ _____

D Rearrange the sentences in chronological order.

1 Mr. Craven had a dream about his dead wife.

2 Mr. Craven went to look for Colin.

3 Mr. Craven fell asleep by a stream in Austria.

4 Colin accidentally ran into Mr. Craven.

5 Mr. Craven went to Austria.

_____ ⇨ _____ ⇨ _____ ⇨ _____ ⇨ _____

Appendixes

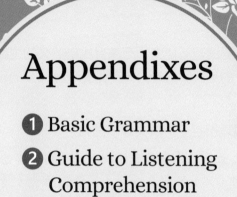

1

Basic Grammar

要增強英文閱讀理解能力，應練習找出英文的主結構。
要擁有良好的英語閱讀能力，首先要理解英文的段落結構。

「英文的閱讀理解從「分解文章」開始」

英文的文章是以「有意義的詞組」（指帶有意義的語句）所構成的。用（／）符號來區別各個意義語塊，請試著掌握其中的意義。

He knew / that she told a lie / at the party.

他知道　　　　她說了謊　　　　在舞會上
⇨ 他知道她在舞會上說謊的事。

As she was walking / in the garden, / she smelled /

當她行走　　　　　在花園　　　　聞到味道

something wet.

某樣東西濕濕的
⇨ 她走在花園時聞到潮溼的味道。

一篇文章，要分成幾個有意義的詞組？

可放入（／）符號來區隔有意義詞組的地方，一般是在（1）「主詞＋動詞」之後；（2）and 和 but 等連接詞之前；（3）that、who 等關係代名詞之前；（4）副詞子句的前後，會用（／）符號來區隔。初學者可能在一篇文章中畫很多（／）符號，但隨著閱讀實力的提升，（／）會減少。時間一久，在不太複雜的文章中即使不畫（／）符號，也能一眼就理解整句的意義。

使用（／）符號來閱讀理解英語篇章
1. 能熟悉英文的句型和構造。
2. 可加速閱讀速度。

該方法對於需要邊聽理解的英文聽力也有很好的效果。
從現在開始，早日丟棄過去理解文章的習慣吧！

以直接閱讀理解的方式，重新閱讀《祕密花園》

從原文中摘錄一小段。以具有意義的詞組將文章做斷句區分，重新閱讀並做理解練習。

Mary Lennox had / a thin little face and a thin little body, / thin light hair and a very sour expression. //
瑪麗‧藍諾克斯有　　　瘦小的臉和身體　　　稀疏的
淡色頭髮和不討喜的表情

She never smiled / – not once / during the long trip / to England. //
她從來不笑　　一次也沒有　　在長途旅行　　去英國

She had come from India / where a terrible disease had killed / thousands of people. //

她來自印度　　　　　　　　那裡可怕的疾病扼殺了
數千人

Among the dead / were Mary's mother and father. //
在死亡的人當中　　　　　　有瑪麗的父母

She didn't miss them / very much / since she hardly knew of them. //
她不會想他們　　　　非常　　　因為她和他們很生疏

Her parents were always away / somewhere / for important business. //
她的父母總是在外　　　　　在某處　　　為了重要商務

Mary Lennox hardly even knew / what their faces looked like. //
瑪麗‧藍諾克斯甚至幾乎不知道　　他們的臉長什麼樣子

Instead of parents, / Mary had servants / that took care of her. //
代替了父母　　　　瑪麗有僕人　　　　照顧她

She only needed to / ask people for / whatever she needed. //
她只需　　　要求別人　　　她需要的任何東西

Unfortunately, / Mary grew up / believing / that everybody was her servant. //
不幸地　　　瑪麗逐漸　　認為　　　每個人都是她的僕人

As Mary walked outside, / she could see tall trees all around. //
當瑪麗走出去時　　　　她可以看到環繞的高聳樹木

There also were flower beds and evergreens / clipped into strange shapes. //

也有花圃和常綠樹　　　　　　　　　　被修剪成奇形怪狀

There were no leaves on trees, / however, / and the flowers were
not blooming yet. //
　　　　　樹上沒有樹葉　　　　　然而　　　　　花兒也還沒綻放

Walking down one path, / Mary noticed a wall / that was covered in
ivy, / but seemed to have no door in it. //
　　沿著一條小路往下走　　瑪麗注意到一道牆　　　覆蓋著常春藤
　　　　　但裡面似乎沒有門

She could see tall trees / behind the wall. //
　　她可以看到高聳的樹木　　　　在牆後

"There must be a gate / along here somewhere," / Mary said. //
　　　一定有一扇門　　　　　在這裡的某處　　　瑪麗說

At that moment, / Mary heard / a robin singing / in one of the trees /
above her. //
　　在那時候　　　瑪麗聽到　　一隻知更鳥在歌唱　　在其中一棵樹上
　　在她上方

As she looked up, / she noticed it jumping / between branches. //
　　當她往上看時　　　　　她注意到牠在跳　　　來往於兩根樹枝之間

It seemed / as if it was trying / to get her attention. //
　　似乎　　　牠好像在嘗試　　　吸引她的注意

Its cheerful singing brought a small smile / to her sad face. //
　　牠令人愉悅的歌聲帶來一抹微笑　　　　在她悲傷的臉上

Guide to Listening Comprehension

 When listening to the story, use some of the techniques shown below. If you take time to study some phonetic characteristics of English, listening will be easier.

Get in the flow of English.

English creates a rhythm formed by combinations of strong and weak stress intonations. Each word has its particular stress that combines with other words to form the overall pattern of stress or rhythm in a particular sentence.

When speaking and listening to English, it is essential to get in the flow of the rhythm of English. It takes a lot of practice to get used to such a rhythm. So, you need to start by identifying the stressed syllable in a word.

Listen for the strongly stressed words and phrases.

In English, key words and phrases that are essential to the meaning of a sentence are stressed louder. Therefore, pay attention to the words stressed with a higher pitch. When listening to an English recording for the first time, what matters most is to listen for a general understanding of what you hear. Do not to try to hear every single word. Most of the unstressed words are articles or auxiliary verbs, which don't play an important role in the general context. At this level, you can ignore them.

Pay attention to liaisons.

In reading English, words are written with a space between them. There isn't such an obvious guide when it comes to listening to English. In oral English, there are many cases when the sounds of words are linked with adjacent words.

For instance, let's think about the phrase "take off," which can be used in "take off your clothes." "Take off your clothes" doesn't sound like [teɪk ɔːf] with each of the words completely and clearly separated from the others. Instead, it sounds as if almost all the words in context are slurred together, [ˈteɪkɔːf], for a more natural sound.

Shadow the voice of the native speaker.

Finally, you need to mimic the voice of the native speaker. Once you are sure you know how to pronounce all the words in a sentence, try to repeat them like an echo. Listen to the book again, but this time you should try a fun exercise while listening to the English.

This exercise is called "shadowing." The word "shadow" means a dark shade that is formed on a surface. When used as a verb, the word refers to the action of following someone or something like a shadow. In this exercise, pretend you are a parrot and try to shadow the voice of the native speaker.

Try to mimic the reader's voice by speaking at the same speed, with the same strong and weak stresses on words, and pausing or stopping at the same points.

Experts have already proven this technique to be effective. If you practice this shadowing exercise, your English speaking and listening skills will improve by leaps and bounds. While shadowing the native speaker, don't forget to pay attention to the meaning of each phrase and sentence.

Step 1 Listen to what you want to shadow many times. Start out by just trying to shadow a few words or a sentence.

 Step 2 Mimic the CD out loud. You can shadow everything the speaker says as if you are singing a round, or you also can speak simultaneously with the recorded voice of the native speaker.

 Step 3 As you practice more, try to shadow more. For instance, shadow a whole sentence or paragraph instead of just a few words.

3 Listening Guide

以下為《秘密花園》各章節的前半部。一開始若能聽清楚發音，之後就沒有聽力的負擔。先聽過摘錄的章節，之後再反覆聆聽括弧內單字的發音，並仔細閱讀各種發音的説明。以下都是以英語的典型發音為基礎，所做的簡易説明，即使這裡未提到的發音，也可以配合音檔反覆聆聽，如此一來聽力必能更上層樓。

Chapter ONE page 14 🎧37

Mary Lennox had a thin little face and a thin little body, thin (❶) (　) and a very sour expression. She never smiled – not once during the long trip to England.
She had come from India where a terrible disease had killed (❷) (　) people. (❸) the dead were Mary's mother and father.

❶ **light hair:** light 和 hair 一起發音時，hair 的 h 音會消失，剩下的 -air 與前面的 light 形成連音 [laɪter]。

❷ **thousands of:** thousands 和 of 連在一起發音時，of 會與 thousands 的 s 產生連音，形成 [sə] 音。因此，thousands of 的發音聽起來像是只有一個字的發音。

❸ **Among:** 重音在第二音節，相對地在重音節前的發音聽起來會較微弱，特別是當重音在第二音節，而第一音節是母音時，第一音節容易被忽略而聽不出正確的發音。

Every day, Mary always did the same things. After breakfast, Mary would walk in the gardens. Often, she would hear the (❶) (   ) the boy crying at night. But she was always told that it was (❷) (   ) (   ).

One day, as Mary was walking in the gardens, she smelled something wet and muddy. It smelled like something living.

❶ **sound of:** of 接在 sound 的後面，of 的 o 會變成 a 的音，產生連音。而 f 的音會省略不發。

❷ **just the wind:** just 與 the 連在一起發音時，just 最後的 t 音會消失，s 音與後面 the 的 [ð] 音產生連音，整句話的重音放在 just 上。wind 的 [d] 音也會帶過，不發出來。

That night, Mary was woken up by the (❶) ( ) ( ).
"That isn't the wind," she said. "I know it isn't. I'm going
to (❷) ( ) where that crying is coming from." Mary
got up and (❸) ( ) a long, dark corridor.

❶ **crying sound again:** sound 與 again 兩個字連在一起唸時，sound 的 [d] 音與 again 的第一個 a 連為 [də] 音。

❷ **find out:** find 的 [d] 音與 out 的 [aʊ] 音產生連音 [daʊ]，out 的 [t] 音會略過不發，聽起來像是一個字的發音。

❸ **walked down:** walked 的 -ed 發 [t] 音，與後面的 down 一起發音時，會省略不發。聽的時候必須注意前後文來判斷動詞的時態。

Chapter FOUR page 68 🎧40

The (❶) ( ), Mary (❷) ( ) Colin's room and
said, "I'm going to see Dickon, but I'll come back."
In five minutes, she was with Dickon in the garden.
When Mary and Dickon started working, she told him
about what Colin (❸) ( ) the night before.

❶ next morning: next 與 morning 合在一起發音時，next 的 [t] 音會迅速略過，聽起來像是沒有發音。

❷ went to: went 與 to 合在一起發音，went 的 [t] 音與 to 的 [t] 音只發一個 [t] 音。

❸ had said: had 與 said 合在一起發音時，had 的 [d] 音會迅速略過，聽起來像是沒有發音。said 的 [d] 音也會略過不發。

Chapter FIVE page 84 🎧41

That spring, the secret garden came alive. The children came alive (❶) (   ). There was a man, however, who (❷) (   ) (   ) in a long time. He had traveled around the world for ten years. But he never felt anything but sadness and boredom. He (❸) (   ) tall man with crooked shoulders and an unhappy face. His name was Archibald Craven.

❶ with it: with 的 th 發音為 [ð]，[ð] 音會與 it 產生連音，產生 [ðɪ] 的音。因此 with it 聽起來像是一個字的發音。

❷ hadn't felt alive: hadn't 的 [t] 音省略不發，felt 的 t 音會與 alive 的 a 音產生 [tə] 的連音。以 t 為字尾的單字如果後面接 a，就會形成 [tə] 的連音。

❸ was a: was 與 a 產生連音，會發出 wasa 的音，聽起來像是單獨一個字的發音。

4

Listening Comprehension

🎧 42 **A** Listen to the CD and fill in the blanks.

1 Don't swim _____ that rock.

2 I don't want to buy that car. It's too _____.

3 Crippled people need to use a _____ to get around the house.

4 The Englishman _____ tea over coffee.

🎧 43 **B** Write down the sentences and circle either True or False.

T F **1** _____

T F **2** _____

T F **3** _____

🎧 44

C Listen to the CD, write down the question and choose the correct answer.

1 _____?

(a) Because he was sick.

(b) Because he caught the flu from her.

(c) Because he was always indoors.

2 _____?

(a) Food and medicine.

(b) Plants and animals from the garden.

(c) Garden tools and seeds.

3 _____?

(a) In a dream.

(b) In the secret garden.

(c) In the river.

45 **D** Listen to the CD and write down the sentences. Then rearrange the sentences in chronological order.

1 _____

2 _____

3 _____

4 _____

5 _____

_____ ⇨ _____ ⇨ _____ ⇨ _____ ⇨ _____

Translation

作者簡介

`p. 4` 法蘭西斯·霍森·伯內特（Frances Hodgson Burnett, 1849–1924）為美國作家，生於英國曼徹斯特。三歲時父親去世，舉家搬至美國。

伯內特為了靠寫作賺錢養家投稿了一篇故事，故事被採用後，她便全心地開始寫作生涯。1886 年，她以次子為模型，出版《小公子》（*The Little Lord Fauntleroy*）。延續此書的成功，伯內特又寫了《莎拉克璐》（*Sara Crewe*）（後改寫為《小公主》（*A Little Princess*））和聞名於世的《秘密花園》（*Secret Garden*）。

伯內特汲取自己永不放棄夢想希望的經歷，克服重重障礙，寫出以樂觀勇氣忍受艱難考驗的角色。當時許多童書旨在傳達道德教義，而伯內特為美國兒童文學帶來轉捩點而備受讚譽。伯內特的作品位居兒童文學的經典地位，以動人可愛的故事持續廣受喜愛。

故事簡介

`p. 5` 《秘密花園》於 1911 年出版，是伯內特的優秀作品之一。內容描述兩個心靈受傷、被世人遺棄的孩子，藉由照顧久疏照料、險成廢墟的牆內花園裡的花朵，找回通往健康心靈之路，因而再生的過程。

克萊文先生住在英國的一座莊園裡，哀傷於妻子的逝世，而將妻子鍾愛的花園上鎖，不許任何人進入。一天，不因失去雙親而泣的小孤兒瑪麗、臥病在床的輪椅男孩柯林，以及鄉村自然環境下成長的強壯鄉下男孩迪肯，發現了遺棄已久的花園。

三個孩子努力讓枯槁的花園恢復新生，終於，花園成為動植物生命蓬勃的天堂。生病的柯林找回健康並開始走路，因兒子的痊癒，沈浸喪妻之痛的克萊文先生也重獲雀躍歡喜。

p. 12–13

瑪麗

我名叫瑪麗‧藍諾克斯。我在印度長大，父母雙亡，所以我和姑丈住在一棟大城堡裡。大部分時間，你會看到我在我的秘密花園裡辛勤工作。這是個非常特別的地方，我在這裡可以結交新朋友、和動物玩耍，享受大自然。

迪肯

嗨，我是迪肯，我喜愛動物，牠們是我的朋友。我大半時間都在密塞威特莊園的花園裡。園藝工作是我最喜歡的嗜好，我覺得每個人都應該要在花園裡從事戶外工作。

柯林

我是柯林‧克萊文，是亞奇伯德‧克萊文的兒子。我病得很重，所以大部分時間都獨自躺在床上。我讀了很多書，但我更希望有朋友可以聊天，一起出去外面玩耍，我已經忘記了有樂趣的感覺是什麼。

亞奇伯德‧克萊文

我名叫亞奇伯德‧克萊文。真令人難過，我的妻子十年前在我們的花園裡過世了。我到世界各地旅行，所以沒有時間陪兒子。我不是故意當一位不盡責的父親，只是一看到兒子就會喚醒我對妻子的思念。

第一章 瑪麗・藍諾克斯

p. 14–15 瑪麗・藍諾克斯的臉和身體都瘦瘦小小的，有著稀疏的淺色頭髮和一張不討喜的臉。她從不笑，就連去英國的長途旅程中也沒笑過一次。

　　她從印度來，那裡流行一種可怕的疾病，使得成千上萬的人喪命，瑪麗的雙親也因此過世了。她和父母很生疏，所以一點也不思念他們。雙親總是在遠地處理重要商務，瑪麗・藍諾克斯甚至不太記得他們的長相。

p. 16–17 瑪麗有僕人們代替父母照顧她。她只需開口，就可以獲得需要的東西。很遺憾，漸漸地瑪麗把每個人都當成了僕人。

　　現在瑪麗的父母都死了，她只剩下唯一的親戚亞奇伯德・克萊文先生。瑪麗對這人一無所知，不過她會住在他家直到十八歲。

　　瑪麗到達英國時，亞奇伯德・克萊文的管家梅德洛太太到港口來接她。

　　瑪麗問道：「你是我的僕人嗎？」

　　梅德洛太太咕噥著說：「欸，你最好注意你的態度！我為你姑丈工作，不是你！我要來帶你去約克郡，那是你的新家。跟我來吧，我們要搭兩點的火車。快一點！」

　　在火車上，瑪麗大部分時間只是望著窗外，看著一幕幕消逝的英國景色，和印度是如此的不同！

p. 18–19 梅德洛太太説：「親愛的，醒來吧。我們已經到了。現在我們要去密塞威特莊園。」

「密塞威特莊園是什麼？」

「那是你的新家，是一座屬於克萊文家的大城堡，已經有數百年之久。城堡旁邊有一個大湖和許多花園。城堡裡有一百個房間，雖然多數都是鎖住的。」

瑪麗問道：「為什麼會被鎖住？」

「克萊文先生喜歡這樣。」

「為什麼？」

「這個嘛，説來話長。克萊文先生有駝背的毛病，造成他性格古怪，年輕時脾氣乖戾刻薄，婚後才有所改變。他太太貌美如花，他深愛著她。

妻子過世後，他變得更加怪異了，把自己鎖在房間裡好幾個月，現在，他偶爾才會出來一下，但很少見人，我想他也不會見你的。」

p. 20–21 他們抵達密塞威特莊園時，瑪麗無法相信自己眼睛所見的。這個城堡比任何她看過或想像中的建築還要大，城堡周圍的花園花兒還沒開放，但仍然很美。

梅德洛太太説：「來吧，瑪麗，我帶你去看你的房間。」瑪麗跟著上了三層階梯，再走過一個長廊來到她房間。屋內壁爐裡的火正燃燒著，桌上已擺設好美味的晚餐。

「這是你的房間，瑪麗。在屋內時你要待在這裡，外頭你就可以隨便閒逛。」

瑪麗説：「好的，女士。」
小女孩坐下來享用晚餐，心中感到一股更甚於從前的孤獨。

p. 22–23 隔天早上，瑪麗被一個叫瑪莎的女傭喚醒。

瑪莎笑容燦爛地説道：「該起床了，來吧，穿衣服了。」

「我不知道要怎麼自己穿衣服。」

「所以囉，現在你該好好學學了。」

瑪麗有一點詫異，但還是生平第一次自己穿好了衣服。

瑪莎幫她準備好豐富的早餐。

「現在，你把它吃完，然後出去外面玩耍。」

瑪麗問：「你不來和我一起玩嗎？」

「不行，從現在起，你要自己一個人玩。假如你運氣好的話，也許會遇到我的小弟弟迪肯。」

「迪肯？」

「沒錯，迪肯是個小男孩，他和動物交朋友。」

瑪麗問道：「我在哪裡可以找到迪肯？」

「噢，他通常都在晃來晃去，也許你可以在花園裡找到他。」

p. 24 「什麼花園？」

瑪莎笑著説：「你問題還真多呢，對不對？我是指莊園周圍的花園，有很多個。但有一個你不能進去，它上鎖了。」

「為什麼它會上鎖？」

「嗯，十年前，克萊文太太在那裡過世的。有天她爬到樹上，從上面摔了下來。之後，克萊文先生就鎖上花園大門，把鑰匙埋在地下。」

瑪麗喜歡秘密花園這構想，對她來説這聽起來既奇異又刺激。

瑪莎說：「你現在出去玩吧。」

瑪麗在外面散步時，可見四周環繞的高聳樹木，也有花圃和被剪成奇形怪狀的常綠樹。然而，樹上沒有葉子，花兒也都還沒綻放。

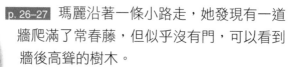

p. 26-27 瑪麗沿著一條小路走，她發現有一道牆爬滿了常春藤，但似乎沒有門，可以看到牆後高聳的樹木。

瑪麗說：「這附近一定有門。」

這時，瑪麗聽到知更鳥在她頭上的枝頭鳴叫。她抬眼一望，看到牠在兩根樹枝上跳來跳去的，似乎在吸引她的注意。愉快的鳥鳴聲，為她悲傷的臉龐添上一抹微笑。

瑪麗回到密塞威特莊園時，心裡不停想著秘密花園的事。她感覺花園一定在她經過的那道牆後面。

p. 28-29 那天晚上，瑪麗坐在床上想著秘密花園的事，聽到一個奇怪的聲音。剛開始，她以為那是風在怒吼的聲音，但是後來發現聲音是從城堡裡傳出來的，聽起來像是男孩在哭。

瑪麗走出房間敲瑪莎的門。

她喊：「瑪莎，瑪莎，我好像聽到有男孩的哭聲。」

瑪莎打開門說：「胡說，那只是風的聲音。」

「但是聲音是從屋內傳來的。」

「才不是，你現在給我馬上回去睡覺。」

那天晚上，瑪麗做了兩個夢，一個是快樂的，她夢到了秘密花園中盛開著玫瑰和野花。另一個是不快樂的，夢裡有一個男孩在哭泣，沒有父母照顧他。

印度的英國小孩

　　瑪麗・藍諾克斯抵達密塞威特莊園時，是個很沒禮貌的小孩。她的行為反映了她在印度的成長方式。1911 年，法蘭西絲・霍森・伯內特寫《秘密花園》小說時，英國掌管了全印度。許多英國人就像瑪麗父母親，去印度幫忙政府治理這國家。

　　多數人過著像國王般的生活，成群印度僕人為他們打理一切。這些英國家庭的小孩過著有如小王子和小公主般的生活。

　　他們有印度僕人服侍，照顧得無微不至，僕人們甚至為小孩穿衣服！難怪有些這裡的小孩會變得嬌寵又懶惰。不過這些小孩可能會感覺被父母忽視，他們的父母通常忙於工作或社交生活，而沒有花太多時間與小孩相處。

[第二章] 秘密花園之路徑

瑪麗每天的生活一成不變，用完早餐後，她會走到花園去玩。晚上，她常聽到男孩的哭聲，但是大家都說那只是風聲。

　　有一天，瑪麗在花園散步，聞到一陣潮濕的泥土味，像是個充滿生命力的味道。

　　她大聲說：「春天來了。」

　　突然，瑪麗聽到一隻鳥在她肩膀上方鳴叫，那是她在莊園第一天看到的知更鳥。瑪麗走向鳥兒，牠卻如瑪麗預期中的沒有飛走。

　　這隻鳥兒站在地上小土堆一個生鏽的環上，看起來很像小狗曾在那裡挖過洞。瑪麗把環從洞裡拔出。

　　她嚷著：「這是什麼？」有一支鑰匙附在環上。

p. 36-37 瑪麗突然間覺得很興奮。她想：「我真想知道這是不是秘密花園的鑰匙。」

然後，怪事發生了。對瑪麗來說，就有如魔法一樣。一陣狂風把牆上的常春藤吹到一旁去，瑪麗清楚看到牆上有圓形門把，門把下有一個鑰匙孔。

瑪麗馬上領悟到這是秘密花園的大門，不然還會是什麼呢？

她的手在發抖，鑰匙差點插不進去孔內。瑪麗四處張望，確定沒有人看到她，然後悄悄溜進去，關起門。

環視四周，瑪麗驚呼：「天啊！」花園聳立的高牆佈滿了玫瑰花莖，玫瑰花叢長滿了整座花園，纏繞在一起。她說：「我一定是在天堂吧。」

p. 38 地上長滿褐色的草，到處都有野花莖，但是瑪麗卻沒看到半點嫩芽。

這座花園很美，但似乎了無生機。也許因為那是瑪麗的私密天地，所以她感覺分外美妙。除了克萊文先生外，沒人知道那裡，而且他也從不到那裡。

瑪麗仔細看著花圃，動手拔除一些樹葉和枯萎的亂枝野草。當她鼻子碰到地面時，看到地上冒出了小小淡綠色的芽。

她說：「這座花園不是完全沒有生命的。」

p. 40-41 那天晚上，瑪麗快樂地回家了。她發現了世界上屬於她的秘密基地，決定要讓那座花園回復生氣。

吃晚餐時，瑪麗突然說：「我想要一個鏟子。」

瑪莎問：「你為什麼要鏟子？」

瑪麗知道她不能說出她的秘密基地。

「這個嘛，這個地方好棒哦，如果我有小鏟子和一些種子的話，我就可以建造一個小花園了。」

「嗯，好主意！你可以寫一封信給我的小弟弟迪肯。他知道哪裡可以買到那些東西，他常常做園藝工作。」

吃完晚餐後，瑪麗寫一封信給迪肯。她把一些錢包在信紙裡，再放入信封。瑪麗興奮地說：「噢，我等不及了！」

p. 42–43 瑪麗來到莊園已經快一個月了。她變得比以前圓潤健康，也快樂多了。

隔天早上，瑪麗得知克萊文先生到奧地利旅行，只留下幾個僕人和瑪麗。

她想：「現在沒有人會來打擾我了。我可以隨心所欲在花園工作。」

那天早上，她沿著小路走到花園時，傳來了奇怪的口哨聲。

瑪麗看到一個男孩坐在樹上，他的肩上有一隻松鼠。有幾隻知更鳥圍繞著他，後腿還蹲坐著的兔子。動物們似乎都在聽這男孩的歌曲。

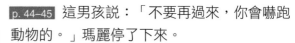

p. 44–45 這男孩說：「不要再過來，你會嚇跑動物的。」瑪麗停了下來。

他說：「嗨，我是迪肯，你一定是瑪麗吧。很高興認識你。我帶來了你需要的園藝工具和種子。」他說話的樣子，好像和她很熟。

瑪麗說：「謝謝，迪肯。我也很高興認識你。你怎麼會有這麼多動物朋友呢？」

「為什麼？因為我自己就是動物呀！來吧，瑪麗，我們一起來栽種吧，你的花園在哪裡？」

　　瑪麗知道她不能永遠保守她的花園祕密。

　　她說：「迪肯，你可以保守秘密嗎？」

　　他說：「我口風很緊的。」

　　「不要告訴任何人喔，我偷了一個花園。」

　　「你說偷了一個花園是什麼意思？」

　　「那是已經上鎖好幾年的花園，克萊文先生說誰都不准進入。我自己發現這花園，因為好幾年沒人照顧，已經死氣沉沉了。」

　　「既然這樣，瑪麗，帶我去花園吧，就只有我能讓它再恢復生氣了。」

　　瑪麗便帶迪肯去秘密花園。

p. 46–47 迪肯四處張望，他和瑪麗一樣看到這花園時，都很吃驚。

　　「這真是個奇妙又美麗的地方！」

　　那天在大太陽底下，他們工作了一整天，清除雜草，把樹葉耙掉。他們栽種種子，拔除枯萎的花朵、給植物澆水，並建造花圃。

　　迪肯看著他們做好的工作，說道：「這裡還有很多工作要做！」

　　瑪麗問道：「你還會再來幫我嗎？」

　　他掛著燦爛的笑容回答：「假如你要我來，我每天都會來。關在這兒，喚醒一座花園，是我人生中做過最有趣的事了。」

　　度過漫長的一天，瑪麗躺在床上，覺得新生活開始了。英國不再是個令人寂寞的地方，它充滿著動物、朋友、花兒，還有一座秘密花園，夫復何求呢？

[第三章] 小克萊文，柯林

p. 50–51 那天晚上，瑪麗又再度被哭聲喚醒。

她說：「那不是風聲，我知道不是，我要去找出哭聲是從哪裡來的。」

瑪麗起床，穿過一條黑暗的長廊，聲音愈來愈大。突然，她看見門扉下透出一道微光。

有人在房門裡哭，聽起來像是小男孩的聲音。

瑪麗打開門，看到一個男孩躺在床上哭，他纖瘦蒼白，一副病容。

男孩一看見瑪麗，大喊：「鬼！鬼！救命阿！」

瑪麗小聲說：「小聲點，我看起來像鬼嗎？」

「看起來不像，那你是誰呢？」

「我叫做瑪麗・藍諾克斯，那你呢？」

瑪麗盯著他的眼睛瞧，他的眼睛是灰色的，在他臉上看來顯得格外地大。

「我叫柯林・克萊文，我是亞奇伯德・克萊文的兒子。」

p. 52–53 瑪麗高興地拍著手說：「太好了，那你就是我的小表弟囉，克萊文先生是我的姑丈。可是為什麼你沒有和爸爸一起去奧地利呢？」

「我從來沒有和他去過任何地方。其實，我也已經很久沒有看到他了。他不喜歡看到我，因為我會讓他想起媽媽。我還是嬰兒時媽媽就過世了，所以我大部分時間都是獨自一個人過。

我的醫生說我不應該和別人接觸，他擔心我會被傳染流行性感冒。假如我能活下去，可能會像爸爸一樣駝背，只是我病得太重，不會活太久。」

瑪麗說道：「我媽媽也過世了，爸爸也是，所以我才會住在這裡。」

柯林問道：「奇怪，我為什麼從來沒有在這附近看過你呢？」

「噢，我大部分時間都在我的花園裡。」瑪麗馬上察覺到她説了不該説的話。

p. 54–55 柯林問道：「什麼花園？」

「噢，那只是一個……一個附近的花園。」

「哪一個？」

瑪麗不想説太多，她怕柯林會告訴其他人花園的事。不過要對表弟撒謊，她心裡很難受，他和她是那麼地相像。

她問道：「柯林，你可以保守一個秘密嗎？」

「應該可以吧，我不知道耶，我以前從來沒有秘密。好吧，如果你告訴我秘密的話，我保證不説出去。」

瑪麗説道：「附近有一個秘密花園，你爸爸禁止任何人進入，所以他把花園的門鎖起來。現在有個名叫迪肯的男孩和我想讓花園恢復生氣。」

當瑪麗説到秘密花園的時候，柯林的眼睛張得很大。他從沒聽過一個這麼驚奇又神秘的地方。

p. 56–57 柯林問道：「瑪麗，你可以帶我去那座花園嗎？我真的很想去。假如有人能幫我把輪椅推到那裡的話。」

「你應該不能離開屋子。」

「可是既然我爸爸出門了，這裡就歸我管。僕人們必須聽從我説的話。」

「我不知道，柯林，我想假如你出去的話，梅德洛太太會很生氣的。」

柯林的臉上看起來很悲傷。

「柯林，假如你身體好一點，也許這樣我就可以帶你出去了。」

柯林雀躍地説：「好的，一定會的。我會好起來，那你一定要帶我去花園。拜託，瑪麗，一定要喔。」

　　那天晚上，瑪麗和柯林聊到很晚，他們聊了許多事。瑪麗告訴柯林在印度的生活是如何，柯林告訴她他覺得自己像是在一個黑暗的房間，只有幾本書作伴。

　　但是他們聊得最多的還是花園的事，柯林想知道花園在哪裡，種了些什麼樣的花，還有那裡有多大。柯林不停地問問題，這男孩很久沒有這麼快樂過了。

　　`p. 58` 隔天下起大雨。瑪麗因為大雨無法出去，便整天和柯林待在一起。瑪莎發現瑪麗在柯林的房間時很生氣。

　　柯林説：「沒關係的，我允許她待在這裡。」僕人不能拒絕柯林的請求。

　　柯林的醫生來時，也一樣覺得很苦惱。

　　「要是被那女孩傳染到流行性感冒怎麼辦？」

　　柯林説：「她不會的，而且她在我身邊時，我感覺身體好多了。」醫生看到事實確實如此，柯林看起來比以前健康。

　　雨下了一個禮拜，瑪麗整個禮拜都和柯林在一起。他的房間不時傳出笑聲。柯林的身體似乎日益強健，他真的很想去花園。

　　`p. 60–61` 這天早上天氣晴朗，瑪麗很早就醒來了，她打開窗呼吸新鮮的空氣。她迅速穿上衣服，跑去花園，迪肯已經在努力工作了。

　　迪肯説：「你看！這花園又有生氣了！」

　　瑪麗四處環顧，是真的！到處都有從地面長出的綠色小芽，玫瑰叢冒出了葉芽，花兒也開了，色彩繽紛，有橘色、紫色、黃色和紅色的。最令人欣喜的是，知更鳥正在築巢。

瑪麗驚訝地問：「這一切是什麼時候發生的？」

「上星期。雨水給花園帶來了滋潤。」

瑪麗很高興看到她以為死去的庭園一片生機盎然。

這天早上，瑪麗和迪肯一起工作時，她告訴他柯林的事。迪肯已經從瑪莎那裡知道這件事。

「大家說克萊文先生清醒時不能看到他，因為他的眼睛看起來真的像極了媽媽。」

「我覺得柯林很可憐，他真的很想要看看這花園。但他卻不能來，因為他病得太重了。」

迪肯說道：「真是太悲慘了，我們一定要帶他一起出來，有我幫他推輪椅就夠了。」

p. 62–63 瑪麗吃完晚餐去看柯林時，柯林很難過。在這美麗的春日，柯林卻一整天都獨自待在屋內。他看起來就如瑪麗第一次看到他時一樣很不舒服。

柯林說：「瑪麗，我想我快死了，再也沒辦法看見你的花園了。」

瑪麗說：「胡說，你只是因為整天待在屋內才會不舒服的，你從沒有呼吸到新鮮的空氣，你要到外面去。」

他說：「不，瑪麗，不行！我的背部長了一個腫塊，我可以感覺得到，你看！」

瑪麗看著他的背。

「柯林，沒有東西呀，那是你想像的。你要來我們的花園工作，愈快愈好。」

他說：「好吧，瑪麗，只要我可以的話，我會和你一起去的。」

然後，瑪麗告訴柯林葉子萌芽了，花兒也開花了。

那天晚上，柯林夢到了那裡的土地和花朵、動物和植物，他夢到了秘密花園。

p. 66-67 英式花園

　　瑪麗住在密塞威特莊園時，愛上了花兒和花園。許多英國人很喜歡花園，他們喜歡在自己的花園種植花草植物，也喜歡參觀像密塞威特莊園這種大宅院的花園。

　　密塞威特莊園反映了英國不同的園藝風格，當瑪麗經過幾座花園要到秘密花園時，她發現花草植物皆有人悉心照顧。

　　英國人最愛在花園草坪嬉戲，像是打網球或保齡球。這裡也有果園，生長著蘋果和梨子等各種果樹。除此之外，許多英國鄉間的宅第還有栽種蔬菜的菜園。

　　秘密花園呈現了十八世紀英國園藝的風潮。那時的英國園丁嘗試讓花園呈現較自然的面貌，以展現大自然的最佳風情。瑪麗‧藍諾克斯正是愛上了這種型態的花園，也發覺了其中的珍貴。

［第四章］我會一直活下去

p. 68-69 隔天早上，瑪麗去柯林的房間，說道：「我要去找迪肯，不過我會再回來。」

　　五分鐘後，她和迪肯在花園開始工作，她告訴他柯林前晚說的話。

　　迪肯說：「在這個春天時光，每個人都應該在外面做事。大家要聽聽鳥叫聲，還有掘土的聲音。假如沒有這樣，就不算活著。我們要趕緊帶他出來，這樣他就會好多了。」

　　瑪麗說：「我有個點子，既然他不能出來，我們可以把花園帶去給他呀！」

p. 70-71 迪肯滿臉疑惑：「這是什麼意思呀？」

「我是説，我們可以從花園帶一些動物和植物給他看。」

「聽起來是個好主意！」

日日夜夜，彷彿都有魔術師來花園變魔術似的。

瑪麗回去坐在柯林床旁，他聞了一聞。

他問道：「這是什麼味道呀？」

瑪麗回答：「這是從花園裡吹來的風。」

隔天早上，瑪麗闖進柯林的房間，嚷道：「春天已經來了，我們打開窗戶吧，柯林。」

瑪麗打開房間所有窗戶，房間充滿鳥鳴聲，清新空氣從窗戶吹進來，她放了兩盆玫瑰在窗台上。

「你不要再想死亡還有你背上的腫塊了，現在你該想著要怎麼讓身體健康起來。進來吧，迪肯。」

迪肯走進房間，説：「哈囉，柯林。」

p. 72-73 柯林對於眼前所見吃驚不已，他興奮得幾乎要從床上跳起來。

迪肯的兩肩上有知更鳥，雙臂抱著一隻小羊，還有一隻小紅狐跟在他旁邊。迪肯把小羊放在地上，兩隻松鼠跑了進來，牠們跳上柯林的床，男孩雀躍地歡呼起來。

柯林此刻決定了今天要去外面走走。

「我需要有人幫我推輪椅。」他説。

「我來，你不必擔心會跌倒。」迪肯説。

然後柯林喚來梅德洛太太，他告訴她：「請告訴所有的僕人我今天要外出，而且從現在開始，如果天氣好的話，我可能都會外出。我外出時，任何僕人都不要跟著我。瑪麗和迪肯會照顧我的，你不用擔心。」

「好的，柯林。」梅德洛太太回答。

p. 74–75 然後柯林做了讓大家都很驚訝的事,他扔開毛毯,把腳放在地上,慢慢地站起來。他的腿不停顫抖,走了短短的五步,又坐回輪椅上,汗流浹背。

他説:「我已經有兩年沒有站起來了。」

迪肯把柯林推到樓梯旁,幫他走下樓梯到外面去。柯林再度靠自己的力量坐回輪椅上。

當柯林的輪椅被推上走道上時,歡欣的淚水從他臉上掉了下來。

最後,他們到達秘密花園的大門,孩子們開始竊竊私語。瑪麗小聲説:「好,柯林,你不能告訴任何人這個地方。」

柯林説:「快點!快點!推我進去!會有人看到我們的!」

當柯林被推進秘密花園後,他驚訝地倒抽了口氣。整個花園生氣蓬勃,繽紛多彩,處處鳥語花香。

p. 76–77 花圃和玫瑰花叢看起來彷彿是畫上去一般,或紫,或藍,或黃,或紅的顏色。玫瑰在他們頭上搭成了橋樑,蜜蜂在花叢裡嗡嗡地穿梭,鳥兒在樹上歌唱。

多少次柯林想像著這花園的樣子,但是他從未想過它會是如此美麗。

陽光灑在柯林臉上,瑪麗注意到他看起來很不一樣,他的臉容光煥發,眼睛閃耀著光芒。

他叫嚷著:「我會好起來的!我會好起來的!而且我會一直活下去!我已經看到春天了,現在我要看到夏天的樣子。我要看到這裡一草一木的成長;我也會在這裡長大。」

那一天,柯林離開輪椅走了幾步,隔天他回來時又多走了幾步。不久他的身體已經強壯許多,可以在花園裡工作了。

p. 78 幾個禮拜過去了，柯林在花園裡辛勤工作。然而，有時他更喜歡坐下來，看著萬物的生長。

有一天，孩子們躺在芬芳的草地上，瑪麗問柯林她一直以來都很想問的問題。

「等你爸爸回來時你要怎麼跟他說？」

「我不會說什麼，我會走向他，讓他看看我現在多麼健康。」

柯林現在和他同年紀的小朋友一樣的健壯。

柯林除了在花園工作外，也開始每天運動。不久後，他變得強壯，似乎也長大了。

p. 80 有一天，柯林丟下鏟子說：「瑪麗！迪肯！看看我！」柯林站得挺直，「記得你們帶我來這裡的第一天嗎？」

迪肯答道：「當然。」

「突然我想起了我那天的樣子，似乎很奇怪，我那時候病得很重，但是我現在是這麼健康！這會是真的嗎？我真的好了嗎？」

「對呀，你好了呀，柯林。」瑪麗答道。

「我是好了，我現在知道，我會一直活下去。我希望爸爸能回家，我想要他現在能看到我的樣子，我也希望媽媽還

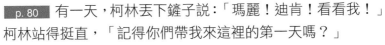

活著，看到我是個多麼健壯的男孩。」

「我想你的媽媽還活著。」迪肯說。

「我想她活在這座花園裡，活在花朵樹木中，活在草地樹叢中，還有活在你心中，柯林。」

135

［第五章］是我，爸爸。

p.84 那個春天秘密花園已恢復生氣，孩子們也跟著活躍了起來。

然而，有一個男人已經很久沒有生命力了。十年來，他環遊世界，但心中除了悲傷和厭倦，別無他物。

他身材高大，肩膀歪斜，一臉愁容。他叫亞奇伯德‧克萊文。

p.86–87 他到每個美麗的地方旅行，但從不在任何地方多停留幾天。他內心傷痛，無心留意身邊的美麗事物。

有一天，怪事發生了。他在奧地利一個美麗山谷裡，山谷很寂靜，他獨自走了一大段路，覺得很累，便在河邊躺下來打個盹。

他睡著時做了一個夢。夢很真實，讓人不覺得那是夢。他聽到有個人在呼喚他，聲音從很遠的地方傳來。

他聽到：「亞奇！」再一次，他聽到比前次更清楚的聲音：「亞奇！」

「莉莉雅絲！莉莉雅絲！是你嗎？」莉莉雅絲是亞奇伯德‧克萊文死去的妻子。「莉莉雅絲！你在哪裡？」

傳回的聲音就像悅耳的歌曲，「我在花園裡。」

然後，夢便醒了。

他醒來時，覺得很平靜也很快樂，他仔細回想夢境，喃喃自語地說：「在花園裡！但是門是鎖著的，鑰匙也被埋了呀。」

p.88–89 亞奇伯德望著小河，看著鳥兒飛過來把頭浸在河裡，喝了水，就飛走了。

他仔細看著一叢野花，葉子被河水濺濕，花朵是深藍色的，這顏色讓他想起了密塞威特莊園旁的湖。

亞奇伯德發現自己看著這些時，彷彿找回多年前看他們的眼神。

他說：「我要回家了。」

在回家長途火車旅行中，亞奇伯德想到了兒子。他發覺自己有十年從沒關心過他了，其實他根本只想要忘記他。他不是故意要當不盡責的父親，但他一點也不算是個父親，甚至很少去看孩子，只有柯林睡著時才會去看他。

亞奇伯德自言自語道：「我是個不盡責的父親，也許我可以改變，也許從現在開始我可以變成一個好父親。」

p. 90–91 火車穿越英國美麗的山谷，亞奇伯德‧克萊文露出了多年未曾綻放的微笑。他心靈平靜，更重要的是他心中抱著希望。他知道他的生活會變好，他知道他會為柯林的生活帶來改變。

亞奇伯德終於返抵家園，他呼喚梅德洛太太。

「我的兒子還好嗎，梅德洛太太？」

「你應該親自去看看，克萊文先生。您一定會很驚訝的。」

「那他在哪裡？」

「他在花園裡，他現在每天都去那裡，其他人都不准靠近那裡。」

於是亞奇伯德走去花園，他走在瑪麗第一天來密塞威特莊園時走的那條路上。

他走到花園的門前停下來，縱使常春藤遮蔽了門，但他還是知道門的位置，只是他忘記把鑰匙埋在哪裡。

「鑰匙會在哪裡呢？」他想道。

p. 92–93 就在當下，他聽到了聲音，似乎是從花園傳來。他聽到孩子們玩耍大笑的聲音。

他想：「奇怪，已經十年沒有人進來花園了。」

突然，亞奇伯德聽到雀躍的叫喊，一位男孩跑出門口，衝進亞奇伯德的懷裡。

他是一位英俊的高個男孩，生命力旺盛。他奇妙的灰色眼睛讓克萊文先生抽了一口氣，他從沒想過這樣的相見。

「噢，你是誰，小男孩？」他問道。

「是我，爸爸！你不認得你的兒子柯林了嗎？」

克萊文先生不敢相信自己的眼睛，他的男孩看起來很健壯，面色紅潤，眼睛明亮，似乎很快樂，看起來一點也不像亞奇伯德認識的那個柯林·克萊文。

「柯……柯林？我不敢相信！真的是你嗎？你看起來很不一樣！」

「那是因為我長大了，爸爸。我不再奄奄一息，開始真正活著了。我恢復了生氣，就像這座花園一樣。我要給你看一些東西，跟我來，爸爸。」

p. 94–95 柯林帶他的爸爸進入花園，花園裡多采多姿，生氣蓬勃，看起來甚至比以前更美麗。花朵的色彩和芳香，讓克萊文先生覺得無比愉悅。

亞奇伯德說：「我還以為這座花園會是一片死寂。」

「剛開始我也是這麼想。」瑪麗說。

「您的姪女瑪麗讓它恢復了生氣。」迪肯說道。

瑪麗說:「迪肯和柯林也有幫忙,再加上一點魔力的助陣,讓一隻知更鳥引導我看到這扇門。」

「然後這座花園讓我恢復了生命力。」柯林說。

然後,他們坐在樹下,柯林告訴他爸爸所有的事。

柯林說:「我再也不要讓這座花園見不得人了,我希望它的大門敞開,讓每個人都能進來。我希望其他生病的男孩也能來這裡,他們也會像我一樣恢復生命力的。」

p. 96-97 然後,亞奇伯德·克萊文和兒子走回城堡,僕人們出來迎接他們。他們仔細看著男孩,發現他已經是另外一個全新的人了。

克萊文先生告訴僕人,花園的牆應該拆除。

這年秋天,花園的面貌又變了。樹葉由綠轉為紅、黃、橘、褐,花朵也枯萎了。

從約克郡來的病童參觀這座花園,開心地看著樹葉飄落下來。他們知道明年花園又會恢復生氣,而且他們也可能會恢復生命力。

Answers

P. 30 **(A)** **①** T **②** F **③** T **④** F **⑤** F **⑥** F

(B) **①** - b **②** - c **③** - d **④** - a **⑤** - e

P.31 **(C)** **①** (b) **②** (c)

(D) **④** → **②** → **①** → **⑤** → **③**

P. 48 **(A)** **①** T **②** F **③** F **④** F **⑤** T

(B) **①** tangled **②** blooming **③** determined
④ amazed **⑤** taken

P. 49 **(C)** **①** The bird was standing on a small mound of earth.
② A gust of wind was blowing aside some ivy from the wall.
③ Her hand was shaking so much that she almost couldn't put the key in the keyhole.

(D) **④** → **①** → **⑤** → **②** → **③**

P. 64 **(A)** **①** F **②** T **③** T **④** T **⑤** T **⑥** F

(B) **①** - e **②** - d **③** - a **④** - c **⑤** - b

P. 65   **C**   ❶ (c)   ❷ (a)

         D   ❶ Dickon is Martha's brother.
               ❷ Mary was awakened by the sound of crying.
               ❸ Mr. Craven locked the garden and buried the key.

P. 82   **A**   ❶ T   ❷ F   ❸ T   ❹ F   ❺ T

         B   ❶ alive   ❷ busily   ❸ shook
               ❹ buzzed, sang   ❺ healthy

P. 83   **C**   ❶ (a)   ❷ (c)

         D   ❹ → ❶ → ❺ → ❷ → ❸

P. 98   **A**   ❶ F   ❷ T   ❸ F   ❹ T   ❺ F   ❻ T

         B   ❶ uncle   ❷ housekeeper   ❸ brother
               ❹ cousin   ❺ maid

P. 99   **C**   ❶ The voice had come back like a beautiful song.
               ❷ But the door had been locked.
               ❸ He hadn't meant to be a bad father.

         D   ❺ → ❸ → ❶ → ❷ → ❹

P. 114　(A)　❶ beyond　❷ rusty　❸ wheelchair
　　　　　　❹ preferred

　　　　(B)　❶ Misselthwaite Manor was the name of Mary's new home. (T)
　　　　　　❷ A robin showed Mary where the secret garden was. (T)
　　　　　　❸ Mary spent a week with Colin because the weather was nice. (F)

P. 115　(C)　❶ Why did Mary think that Colin felt bad? (c)
　　　　　　❷ What did Dickon and Mary bring Colin? (b)
　　　　　　❸ Where did Archibald Craven see his wife? (a)

　　　　(D)　❶ Mary found the secret garden.
　　　　　　❷ Mary and Dickon brought Colin to the secret garden.
　　　　　　❸ Archibald Craven met his son near the secret garden.
　　　　　　❹ Mary came to Misselthwaite Manor.
　　　　　　❺ Mary met Colin.

　　　　　　< ❹ → ❶ → ❺ → ❷ → ❸ >

Adaptor of *The Secret Garden*

David Desmond O'Flaherty

University of Carleton (Honors English Literature and Language)
Kwah-Chun Foreign Language High School,
English Conversation Teacher

秘密花園【二版】
The Secret Garden

作者 _ 法蘭西斯・霍森・伯內特
　　　（Frances Hodgson Burnett）

改寫 _ David Desmond O'Flaherty

插圖 _ Petra Hanzak

翻譯／編輯 _ 劉心怡

作者／故事簡介翻譯 _ 王采翎

校對 _ 王采翎

封面設計 _ 林書玉

排版 _ 葳豐／林書玉

播音員 _ Amy Lewis, Michael Yancey

製程管理 _ 洪巧玲

發行人 _ 周均亮

出版者 _ 寂天文化事業股份有限公司

電話 _ +886-2-2365-9739

傳真 _ +886-2-2365-9835

網址 _ www.icosmos.com.tw

讀者服務 _ onlineservice@icosmos.com.tw

出版日期 _ 2019年11月 二版一刷（250201）

郵撥帳號 _ 1998620-0 寂天文化事業股份有限公司

國家圖書館出版品預行編目資料

秘密花園 / Frances Hodgson Burnett原著；
Davie Desmon O'Flaherty改寫. -- 二版. --
[臺北市]：寂天文化, 2019.11
　　面；　公分. -- (Grade 3經典文學讀本)
譯自：The secret garden
ISBN 978-986-318-855-1(25K平裝附光碟片)

1. 英語　2. 讀本

805.18　　　　　　　　　　　108017939